GREEN GRASS FEVER

Charles Flynn

MINERVA PRESS

LONDON

MIAMI   RIO DE JANEIRO   DELHI

GREEN GRASS FEVER
Copyright © Charles Flynn 2001

All Rights Reserved

ISBN 0 75411 499 6

First Published 2001 by
MINERVA PRESS
315–317 Regent Street
London W1R 7YB

Printed in Great Britain for Minerva Press

GREEN GRASS FEVER

For my pretty friend who is also well read

Charlie

Preface

In 1952, those people living in the land of the brave and the home of the free were shocked by the Russian premier, Nikita Khrushchev's boast of 'We will bury you' and then, during the next four years, his proceeding to strategically position long-range bombers throughout the Soviet Union 'for defensive measures'. Such belligerence was deemed a threat to every God-fearing American. Senator Taft of Ohio announced that 'America must be fortressed to preserve the Gibraltar of western civilization' and President Eisenhower added his endorsement with a joint message to Congress instructing the military to escalate defense spending. Nuclear-powered submarines, U2 spy planes and long-range search radar were the deterrents to which America turned. The largest hole in the wall of the western Gibraltar fortress was the North Pole.

The high Arctic presented no obstacle to long-range bombers or intercontinental missiles for that matter. The Americans turned to their Canadian neighbors for assistance.

It was agreed that a 'Distant Early Warning System' would be beneficial to both nations, the Americans would gain twenty minutes for retaliation or prayer or whatever and the Canadians, with the help of all those American bucks, would be closer to balancing the national debt. The agreement at which Washington and Ottawa arrived was that America would supply materials, engineering and money: Canada would supply land and the manpower to operate the system. The American generals only agreed to the use of Canadian civilians with the proviso that there be American supervisors and, in addition, Canadians had to be trained in American military procedures and further, that Canadians would be finely screened and checked for 'Red' affiliations. Federal Electric Company of Paramus, New Jersey, was awarded the operational contract and a coast-to-coast search for super-technical-type Canadians began.

American know-how swung into high gear and twenty-seven months later, high-speed data was moving from the Arctic ice cap to the American military brain center at Colorado Springs. The folks at home could stop worrying about unexpected company walking in uninvited. They now had a super buzzer on the back door.

Chapter One

Located ninety miles south of the Chicago Dearborn Street Railway station is Streator, Illinois, (population 36,000), the town selected as an ideal location for an air-search training school. The determining factor was the high volume of air traffic in and out of O'Hare and the convenient ring of air force bases in Iowa, Missouri, Michigan and Indiana. There were so many aircraft in the skies above Streator that southbound geese detoured and flew Ohio air.

The small, centrally located railway center had slowly retired from the limelight as an Al Capone drinking hole. The main action had moved on but in 1962 there were still fifty-three bars and saloons open seven days a week from 10:00 A.M. to the wee hours of tomorrow. If the need arose, these 'licensed' premises could provide bar seating for every man, woman and child in La Salle county. A small exaggeration, but the fact remained that no registered voter ever needed to stand to imbibe within the town limits of Streator.

On Sunday, August 20, 1962, the Santa Fe Super Chief, en route from New York City to Los Angeles, pulled in to Streator for a routine five-minute stop. Twenty-eight Canadians reluctantly decamped the luxury of continental travel and in groups of four and five were taxied to a downtown, four-storied, 1920 vintage hotel, known locally as the 'Tilton Hilton' but to anyone who stayed over a weekend it was 'The Hutch'. The Canadians milled about the marble-columned lobby as the busy desk clerk assigned rooms, three or four men to a room.

'Holy Christ! Do I look like I need three guys to tuck me in?'

'I'm sorry, Mr. Sawchuck.' The clerk's voice was drowned out by the roar of Jake's.

'I need a room… alone! I haven't bunked up since the navy and even then my snores kept the top watch awake.'

'I'm sorry, sir, but the arrangements have been made. Federal Electric made reservations for each man.' The desk clerk checked his registration list. 'Mr. Sawchuck, you're assigned to Room 309 with Mr. Clow, Mr. Dempster and Mr. Rafferty. There is nothing I can do. Please, sir, see the manager in the morning. Perhaps he can help you.'

The clerk turned his attention to the next man, leaving Jake to find his way to the third floor. When the new 'bunkies' arrived, Jake grinned and stuck out a big, open hand to a happy-looking Michael Clow.

'Irish, damn my eyes, Michael *Irish* Clow. Where did you come from? Were you on that train? Damn, you're a sight for sore eyes.' The bear-sized Jake grabbed the smaller man's hand and pumped it with enthusiasm. 'Michael Clow. I should have caught the name. You still have that mop of red hair. Jeez, it's been a long time since Turkey. How ya been?' Turning to the other two men in the doorway and offering his big hand, Jake became the welcoming host. 'Hi. Come on in. I'm Jake Sawchuck.'

'Aaron Dempster. Good to see you.' Aaron's hands were full with a suitcase and guitar and he was busy looking for a corner in which to drop the load but he nodded towards the fourth roomy. 'The guy behind me calls himself Doc.'

The silver pince-nez glasses nodded. 'Hi. So you're the Sawchuck. I'm the guy in Greece you talked to all night. We were doing the Turkey to Greece radio lineup.'

Jake took another look at the last man, stocky, bow tie, red cheeks on an apple-shaped face and the silver glasses. He embodied the characteristics of an old-timey medicine man.

'Doc. You're Doc. Sure as hell I'd know that voice. Fourteen hours before we got off the phone that day. How ya been?'

The men moved their suitcases in, claimed their beds and began the process of a close living-quarters existence. In a short time there was agreement about who would squat where and it was Doc who suggested that solids were needed. Food, some form of sustenance: perhaps some nectar.

'A good place to eat?' the now idle desk clerk repeated. 'Sure, Rokies, across the street. Not fancy but good food. Not bad for this town.'

Rokies's main attraction was a five-piece, Dixie band. Their stage was the raised area in the center of the U-shaped bar. The menu was short: steaks, bacon and eggs, steak and eggs, or eggs. Like the desk clerk said, 'Good, not fancy, but not bad for this town.'

When the steaks had been devoured and with fresh drinks in hand and the music taking a twenty-minute break, the four men sat back, relaxed, at ease coming down from the hard traveling of the past twenty hours.

Michael opened the talk with: 'Where you from, Aaron? I know you from some job down the road, don't I?'

'I was about to ask you the same,' Aaron said. 'I know your name. Were you with GE two or three years ago?'

Michael nodded. 'Ya, two years ago. The TD-2 run-up.'

Jake cut in. 'GE. That rings a bell… in the Maritimes. Were you down there? How did you wind up here?'

Michael chuckled aloud. 'Funny thing. I was up a telephone pole fifty miles south of Calgary. Seems like ten thousand miles from here.'

Michael 'Irish' Clow was belted to the top of a forty-foot telephone pole. It was three o'clock in the afternoon and it had been twelve thirty when he strapped on the climbing spurs, buckled the wide safety belt around his waist and climbed to his lofty perch. The view was of a flat sun-browned prairie, no frills, no oohs and aahs. To hell with the blue sky and puffy white clouds. Michael was standing with knees locked, ass hanging, sore-footed, sore-backed and with a full bladder doing what he described as a 'beer money indentured job'. Any enjoyment of the fresh-air perch had boiled away in the afternoon sun. Below him, Bingo Siveck was dozing against the side of the truck, enjoying the relative comfort afforded by being at ground level. Michael tested the last pair of wires and began wrapping up in preparation for the return to earth. Below him, Siveck answered a call on the mobile radio.

'It's for you, Irish. Division office. You want to take it now or will you call them when you get down here?'

'I'll call them from here.' Michael clipped a service phone across a handy pair of wires and dialed. The conversation was brief. The serenity of the summer afternoon was destroyed by the raucous yells of a gone-wild Michael. He was still hollering when he landed on the ground by the perplexed Bingo.

.

'I got it! I got the job with Federal Electric, the DEW-line job.' He grabbed the open-mouthed Bingo by the shoulders and spun him around. 'You hear me? I got the job with Federal.'

Siveck shook him off, stepped back out of reach, grinning in response to his friend's exuberance. While Michael was shucking out of the safety belt-load of tools and relieving himself of the thigh-high spur irons, Bingo was reviewing the situation. He and this young guy had been partners for eight months. They were a good team. This Mike Clow was okay, twenty-three, five foot eight, solid build and sharp. Smarter than the average ya-hoo. Not much time wasted with conversation and he knew electronics. Also knew wire line and did his share plus on every job. A good partner.

'So you got the job but what about right now?'

'Well, Bingo old buddy, we go to town. I draw my time. Buy you a beer or two or three, then I catch a bus to Calgary. I have an interview with the Federal Electric personnel guy tomorrow morning at ten o'clock. Guy named Lumly. Ed Lumly.'

Bingo, noticeably less exuberant than the jubilant Michael, offered prudent advice. 'Whoa up a minute. Sure you can dump this job, there's no problem about that. This wire line shit is going the way of the dinosaur but you're not going to get paid off today. Payroll will take their own time about the paperwork. What I'm thinking, now don't take this personal, what I figure is that this don't sound like no guaranteed job. You say you got an interview but that's still a day's walk from the company lunchroom, so I say, don't be in no big hurry to quit.'

'What the hell, Bingo. I'll get it. I'm a "been there done that com-technician". I've worked on the Trans Canada system, the TD-2 sites. I was with GE when I did site testing in Turkey and I've installed and commissioned God knows how many channels of the GEC SPO50/52 mux gear. You saw the help-wanted ad and the qualifications requirements. Hell, they might as well been writing my resume.'

Bingo nodded agreement. 'Sure, I saw it. Big money, technical jobs in the high Arctic, but there'll be a thousand guys applying.'

'You're right about that, Bingo, but they've already done the weeding, that's why the guy phoned me. The ones they don't want will get a form letter. You know the routine. "We will keep your application on file." Right?'

'You got a point there. Ya, you may be headed north.'

Michael drained his now warm beer and finished his hiring narrative with a big grin and a 'Here I am. No more climbing spurs, no more wire line. How about you, Aaron? Where did you get hired?'

'It was in Toronto, and it was different. A little hectic, hurried, whatever.'

Jake asked if anyone had explained what the *job* was, to which Aaron nodded and said, 'Ya. A bit about Radar and Troppo Scatter.'

Aaron Dempster was ten minutes late for the Federal Electric job interview. He had half-walked, half-run from the parking lot and now he sat, breathing hard, a film of sweat bathing his face and soaking the back of his shirt, and to add to the screw-up, these two clowns had lost his resume or the file with his application for employment. The hotel room drapes were pulled back and the window was open in a vain effort to siphon off stale cigarette smoke. The bright glare of full sunshine shone directly on Aaron's face. This interview was getting to be a royal pain.

Ed Lumly and Harry Devon, the Federal Electric personnel officers, sat facing Aaron with their backs to the open window, busily sorting brown folders scattered across the top of the coffee table. One or the other of the men occasionally tried to reassure Aaron with small talk.

'It's here, Aaron, your file. Had it a minute ago.' Aaron nodded his head and forced a smile. No call to be surly. It was going to be a long day. He had already been waiting fifteen minutes.

Ed Lumly looked up from the clutter and said, 'Aaron! You okay? You look a little pale.'

Aaron was saved an inane remark about hurry up and wait by Harry who said, 'Got it. Knew it was here.' He glanced through the file before passing it to Lumly.

Lumly nodded his head and said, 'Okay, Aaron. Here's your application and head office approval to hire.'

Aaron visibly relaxed and sat forward in his chair to say, 'That's great. Thank you. Thank you very much.'

Harry said, 'Welcome aboard, Aaron. We're glad to have you. We hire a lot of techs and we think you will fit our job requirements nicely. Ed, would you give Aaron a brief rundown on the job and the immediate arrangements.'

'Sure. This is a posting to the high Arctic, above the Seventy-fifth Parallel. It is the most remote area in the world and because of the high degree of isolation we'll pay top dollar and a hardship allowance. Six-day work week and time and a half after forty hours. The work sites are remote and the contract will require that you spend six months on site before taking any leave. You can have three weeks' vacation after a six-month tour and when you have worked a year there will be a thousand-dollar bonus and another three weeks R and R. The high Arctic is isolation with a capital I. It's a demanding job but in no way do we consider it hazardous. Primarily, this is electronic surveillance. Okay? First thing, we send you to Streator – Streator, Illinois, where you will spend six weeks at our training school doing a refresher course on the Doppler radar you serviced during your air-force days. Any questions?'

Aaron shook his head and Ed Lumly continued.

'We'll show you some sophisticated design changes involving the broadband carrier and there are some impressive tropospheric scatter transmitters for you to play with. Think of it as graduate school. We want you to look over some mobile radio schematics, some test equipment servicing and then there will be a day or two on powering up a diesel generator, polishing floors and several other mundane jobs but before you get to be a "know it all" the school director will post you to a DEW-line site. Okay? Can you handle it? Any questions?'

Aaron had lots of questions but the immediate one was, 'When do I leave?'

'This is abrupt but we want you to take a medical tomorrow morning at eight o'clock. We have reservations for you to fly to Chicago the day after. You'll arrive in Streator on Sunday afternoon and classes begin Monday morning. Any problems? Good. Welcome aboard.'

Jake ordered a round of beer and when it was on the table he discussed his hiring.

'It wasn't much. Took ten minutes. They handed me a plane ticket and here I am.'

He had timed his hiring time including the entry and exit: nine minutes and thirty-five seconds. Jake had spent a minute in front of Room 411, his big hands checking buttons and pocket bulges, then, after a loosening shake of the shoulders, he knocked. The door was immediately opened by a short, gray-haired man who smiled and extended his right hand in greeting.

'Good morning. I'm Harry Devon. You must be Jake Covlin.'

In the hotel room, Jake was introduced to Ed Lumly who said, 'Morning, Jake. Would you like a coffee? Cream and sugar on the table.'

Jake poured coffee and lowered himself into a chair. Ed Lumly was the senior personnel officer for Federal Electric. An astute man, well-practiced in making quick accurate assessments of the men he interviewed. He had studied Jake's resume and was impressed: two years' study of electronics at Ryerson Technical Institute; four years with the Canadian Navy, with two years of special training in search radar; three years of field engineering with RCA where he had specialized in the newly emerging microwave communication systems. Exactly the qualifications Federal was looking for but now Federal needed to know if Jake could function within their job parameters.

'Why did you leave RCA?

'They ran out of work, Mr. Lumly, after bidding low on some major jobs. It was getting close to quit or take a part-time "call you when we need you" deal and I like to think I'll decide when I need unemployment.'

Lumly grinned and thought, Their loss is our gain, and then aloud asked, 'Can you start today?'

Jake answered, 'I'm your man.'

Jake drained his glass of beer and repeated his earlier statement. 'It wasn't much. Handed me a ticket, shook my hand and here I am.'

Rafferty had sat quietly, enjoying the company and the camaraderie and now he added his opinion. 'It was not the speedy dispatch of the hiring that impressed me. It was with the damned inconvenience of it. I had a lot going for me that morning.'

In Vancouver, the Federal Electric request for Doc's presence was inopportune. Doc – Christian name, Stanley – Rafferty had been moving on a tight schedule. The desk clerk at the Hyatt Regency had intercepted Doc's double-quick 12:45 P.M. leave-taking by pressing into his reluctant hand a brown registered business envelope, addressed to Rafferty and marked personal. Doc's tight schedule was interrupted further when his racetrack-bound taxi was delayed by a long red light at Hastings and Doc used the idle time to open what might have been a check. The formal letter advised Doc that an interview had been arranged on his behalf and that he was expected to present himself, punctually, at 1400 hours at a nearby hotel. Doc frowned, sighed and swore and swore again. 'Military, goddamn military.' To the cab driver he added, 'Change of address, buddy. Take me to the Bayshore.'

Doc was annoyed, bugged, browned-off. He had spent the morning with coffee pot, cigarettes and the morning track sheet. He had without a doubt picked the day's eight winners, well, five for sure, and now this: employment. Doc had spent the past eleven weeks in the pursuit of paid-up pleasure.

Doc was a five-year veteran of the Canadian Air Force. He had qualified as a radar tech at Clinton, moved on to graduate study at Trenton and had then taken his master goof-off at Baden-Baden. Germany was a short step to the green pastures of the RCA field engineering team.

His last assignment was a year in Turkey where he had accumulated a fat bankroll and a desire for a more relaxing lifestyle. Seventy-five days had reduced the fat bankroll to walk-around money and the relaxing lifestyle was becoming more hassle than relaxing. It was time for gainful employment, another stake, something more substantial. Perhaps the relaxing lifestyle required more R and D (research and development) and then, by God, lookout. After all, money is only a commodity, like hog bellies or malt whisky. It's the knowing how and a small dash of luck.

At the Streator bar, Doc nodded his head and repeated his assertion.

14

The hiring process had been quick.

'It was brief, very brief. Five minutes, ten tops. I was on my way to the track with a sure thing. Ed Lumly, you met Ed? Ed was, ah, astute, very astute. When I explained about *Storm Warning*, a horse in the third, well, Ed and I, we negotiated a contract in five minutes.'

Actually it was seven minutes. Ed had ascertained that Doc was anxious to work in the Arctic, even desperate. Doc signed the necessary papers and twenty minutes later he was laying out twenty bucks on *Storm Warning*. He should have saved his money.

There were some grins and chuckles. The last of the beer was drunk and someone said something about 'morning coming early'.

Chapter Two

Perched on a two-hundred-foot, red and white radio tower, a twelve-foot, slice of lemon-shaped Doppler radar antenna was the signpost marking the location of the training school. Surrounded by miles of precisely arranged Illinois cornfields, the school itself was an amorphous collection of interconnected Quonset huts.

The men, enrolled for the Hands in Educational Advancement, were there because they had proven a superior ability in their chosen discipline, electronics, and the present situation was something like teaching a duck about water. The men were not only familiar with the equipment, but they had often been involved with the design and development. The detailed review of the well known became tedious and relief was found in the Streator nightlife, more specifically, in the Streator bars, a dozen of which could be found within crawling distance of the 'Tilton Hilton'. There were good days when the course would grab the men's attention, such as an in-depth study of rainfall, weather balloons, weather patterns, clouds, barometers, wind speeds and snow classifications. At one of the better three-hour sessions arctic survival was plumbed in depth. Staying alive without shelter in forty below darkness captures a lot of people's attention. The lecturer had spent two years on the line but when pressed for details, his replies were vague generalizations.

'There are no trees, no coconuts, no roses and no green grass,' he told them, 'but there sure is a hell of a lot of frozen water.'

During another session, the company's working directives were reviewed. A lot of talk developed about the company policy of no fraternization, especially with the female natives. This would be grounds for immediate termination. If a man was struck with severe lower abdomen pain, a dimming of the eyesight and hand tremors, in other words, an acute case of horny, the victim would avail himself of the use of a cold shower. No other treatment would be tolerated. Even today there are X number of DEW-liners who suffer mixed feelings about a running shower. The company rules and regulations moved some of the recruits to seek more civilized working conditions. The remainder of the class were duly processed and assigned work sites with strange-sounding names: Pin Three, Bar Four, Cam Two, Foxe One, or the ominous-sounding Dye One.

Michael, Jake, Aaron and Doc wrapped up the American adventure, the Streator bullshit and ballyhoo and with achy heads made their way to the DEW-line bosom – Hangar Nine, Winnipeg International Airport.

Chapter Three

The four repatriated Canadians spent a day in Winnipeg recovering. A day of convalescence. Time to revitalize after the satiety of American booze and American broads, the original American B and B. The last free day was spent in the privacy of individual rooms having individual thoughts, and they arrived at Hangar Nine showing few of the signs of their recent dissipations, looking almost healthy. Ready for action: a gung-ho group. They took up positions at the tail end of a short line.

At 10:00 A.M. they were allowed admittance to Stan, the bookkeeping-man's empire; a white clickity-clackity office where Stan, his shining glasses reflecting a lot of the overhead fluorescent lights, locked them into a world of paper forms. The file clerks and the typists, all Stan's assistants, worked up individual forms declaring next of kin, burial plans, life insurance, payroll deductions, income tax withholdings, and the 'Super Gold Star' secrecy act, which they swore to with hands on the Bible. When the papers were signed – press hard, four copies – Stan, with a full Pepsodent smile, shook their hands and offered a welcome aboard to each man.

The men were then directed to Equipment and Supply where they were fitted with a full suit of arctic clothing by a mall fox-quick man who answered to the name of Aggie. Communication with Aggie was conducted in a loud voice through a hole-in-the-wall arrangement in the waiting room. Aggie could always be found in the supply room, surrounded by bins of parkas and mukluks: 8:00 A.M. or midnight. When he was not supplying, he sat, chair tilted back, feet up, engrossed in that day's horoscope or track sheet. Each man received as standard issue a six-pound sleeping bag, an Arctic, deep-cold parka, insulated flight pants, mukluks and liners, elbow-high lined mitts, sunglasses, a fur-lined cap and miscellaneous lesser items. Each item would be charged against a newly opened account and as Aggie pushed the pile through the window, each northbound body would pack this bulky blue, green and gray-colored mess into a large zippered flight bag, sign Aggie's detailed inventory form and forever more be accountable to Aggie.

By two o'clock the registration was complete. The men were informed that their northbound chariot was scheduled to depart at 2100 hours and that they would return to Hanger Lane no later than 2000 hours. Be punctual or be unemployed. The new employees called a yellow cab and headed downtown. Aggie had imparted the name of a better-class bar that had a 'nice atmosphere'. The men were quiet on the ride, people watching: people at bus stops, people in crosswalks, people in a hurry, people staring in store windows. The men gathered memories. Memories of faces, great legs, a cute ass, a marvelous pair of tits or blue eyes framed by red hair. It might be a long time until the next girl.

The bar was jumping. Vacationing DEW-liners on a last-day whoop-up, regaling greenhorns with near truths and out and out bullshit. The newly processed foursome found an empty table in the beer-smell atmosphere of the dimly lit drinking hole. The bartender dispatched refreshments by means of a short-skirted hostess and the first round was 'on the house'. Norse, the bartender, claimed to remember the face of every customer and he did it very well, especially with the twenty-dollar tippers. Norse had it made, for another year of twice-a-week DEW-line crews heading in or out from Cambridge Bay or Cape Dyer, leaving large tips in passing, and Norse could retire from the demands of the public and raise bees or cows.

Back in yesteryear, Winnipeg had been the ox-cart dispatch center of the western Canadian settlement movement. A church, next the railway, followed by a one-room school, then the university, Eatons and Woolco shopping. Historically, the town showed satisfactory growth and after 1960, the yearly US$16 million air-force DEW-line contract gave Winnipeg the seed money for Red River flood control dykes, downtown rebuilding, and whilst we're at it, an annex on the Airport Inn and another twenty blocks of pavement for Portage Avenue.

Hell, them DEW-line people just keep a-coming. The town liked DEW-liners.

When the clock reached 1930 hours, the men cleaned up the last of the drinks and, helping those whose lower extremities had been weakened by all the sitting, took taxis to the unadorned Hangar Nine waiting rooms.

At 2000 hours, twenty-nine of the thirty men listed in the manifest had assembled in the hangar's waiting room. Security had checked names and ID's. Told them to move along to the waiting room and park it. There might be some delay. Impersonal. 'We've done this before' professionalism. By 2200 hours, all thirty were present and waiting, resigned to the fact that a weather front north of Churchill would keep the flight grounded for a 'short time'.

The waiting room was a wide hallway to which doors had been added. Three large lights had been hung from a dark ceiling to brighten up the green and yellow walls. The entrance door and the supply-room window were propped open. The departure gate sported a large sign: NO ADDMITTANCE. EXIT ONLY. Mounds of sleeping bags, parkas and personal effects were scattered between groups of standing men. Three of the men, a bit the worse for wear, had claimed large sections of the waiting-room benches for sleep. A few of the men, used to the 'hurry up and wait' routine, were dozing against the walls, while others prowled up and down the aisles.

Several groups were smoking, small-talking, everybody subdued, quiet, hung-over. Earlier in the day each man had been fitted with an Arctic kit. The Arctic kit and personal baggage would be hand-carried on board. The flight clothes would be worn by the men because the plane might decide it had flown far enough and do an immediate landing.

Michael was one of those standing pensively and quiet. With him were Aaron and Jake. Now, bored with conducting a detailed examination of the bare walls, Jake murmured something and walked out, heading for the toilets. Shortly, thereafter, Aaron and Michael followed, past the closed and locked offices. Doc, perched on the edge of a sink, had been expecting the arrival of these three and he opened the small talk.

'What's the latest on the flying machine, Michael?'

'I hear it'll be another hour.'

'Damn these birdheads. Sometimes I think pilots forget where they park.'

Aaron interrupted a 'reach for the ceiling' stretch to remark, 'If

I spend much more time in this hole, they'll be sending me to a funny farm.'

Doc said, 'They may do that, buddy, they may do that.' Doc handed Aaron a half pint of rye, which he then passed around. When the bottle returned to Doc, he finished the remainder, and tossed the empty bottle into a garbage bin.

It had been two months and now they had been tested, screened and had their names run through the American security checks. They had been hired with the understanding that the job would be theirs only after the successful completion of the job-related courses at Streator. So now what? They were permanent staff, no doubt about that – laminated card; employee number; admittance to the inner sanctum. Wow!

The Streator, Illinois site was built as the prototype of an operational DEW-line station and the training program, the 'hands-on familiarization', should have been on-the-job training but the 'as is built' was a British Second World War air command post with related training.

Doc summed up the ineffective six-week stay with the succinct, 'We flew to Chicago on a Sunday and went into some kind of a time warp.'

At 2300 hours a loud clang, the result of a large boot being applied to a non-functioning coffee machine, causes a ripple of movement. A small buzz of hushed talk, a banged door outside the ugly waiting room and some of the men began the positive action of assembling in front of the NO ADDMITTANCE. EXIT ONLY door. An airline employee in blue uniform announced that boarding could proceed. 'Please do not leave any personal belongings in the waiting room.'

Chapter Four

A four-engine DC-4 had been parked in an adjoining hangar a short walk from the waiting room, through the long black shadows to the boarding steps. The detachment of departing men filed on to the plane, dragging stuffed flight bags, bulging suitcases and a battered guitar, much like small boys boarding the summer camp bus. A huge mound of freight, mailbags and burlap-wrapped machinery parts filled the forward passenger section and, in the space that remained, the freight crew, with pathological mentality, had bolted to the floor, thirty-two worn-out seats, leaving exactly sixteen inches of space between each row as a concession to comfort. There remained nine feet of empty floor space where the men dumped their 'hand carry' arctic kits. One hour north of Winnipeg and this area would be better used for a game of five-card stud.

The passengers squeezed themselves along the narrow aisle into the closely packed seats. When all the bodies were firmly compressed into their allotted space, the metal doors clanged shut, engines whirred, whined and roared and the planeload of folks and cargo taxied out to the end of the airport acreage and parked. Some of the men grew highly vocal about this further delay. Doc remarked that the pilot had lost page two from the 'how to fly an airplane' book but more speculation along these lines was drowned out by the engine noise as the pilot began pre-flight checks.

Obscenities about the noise were hurled at the forward cabin but the engine roar grew ever louder as the airplane driver goosed the engines, a primitive declaration of power, or a challenge to other DC-4s to race. The plane's engine noise reached a headachy din and at last the plane began to move. Slowly, the plane tested its strength, preparing for flight; rattling and shaking, feeling its way along the concrete strip, and gradually the candle-sized runway lights blended, becoming a luminous white line. The lines of light dropped beneath the wing, blending with a grid of white lines stretching from black horizon to black horizon and above, a dark-blue velvet glistening with the flicker of infinite stars.

Michael came back to a conscious level at 4:00 A.M. with a king-sized head, a desert-sized thirst and buckled into a spring-dead, cloth-covered, wooden milking stool, equipped with a straight back. Beside him Jake and Aaron suffered similar agonies, for they sat, glassy-eyed and quiet, the engine noise impeding small talk. Doc had found some measure of relief in the poker game on the floor by the emergency exit door.

The oval windows, black mirrors during the long hours of night, now became translucent and in a short time the opaque view beyond the small window cleared and became a haphazard pattern of blue and white. Small clouds floated alongside and below, much like a large pail of popcorn that had been spilled across a dark-blue rug. Stretched from horizon to horizon the white-spotted blue sky was a pale copy of the white-spotted blue sea. An intense red spot in the east blossomed, forming a brilliant red arc and even as they watched, the fire spread, up and out along the full length of the horizon. Below, the popcorn-covered blue rug turned black with long white jagged cracks stretching to the edge of the distant rim.

The cutesy flight girl served an ugly-looking fluid that tasted more like cardboard than coffee. In the tail, a dozen guys were lined up, waiting to use the 'can'. It was not a long wait, for any delay behind the door earned a vocal 'Move it, cowboy' or a threat of bodily harm from the sour, rumpled, waiting line. The 'can' was a small three-foot-square cupboard that lurched and jerked with every movement of the plane's tail. The thigh-high commode had been missed more than once and the place stunk. Small, green, packaged, wet-wash tissue packs had been dumped in the sink, and several dozen were scattered on the floor with the remains of the ass-wipe roll. The end of the roller towel was pushed up in a bundle under the sink and some sad case was yelling, 'Hurry up.' Aaron rethought the idea of a morning rinse. Back at the seat the boys poked at what looked like a plastic breakfast with a plastic fork on a plastic tray.

The big, four-engine plane droned north. Two hours, two days, the numb bodies squirmed, stretched, twisted and eventually a report that 'We'll be there in ten minutes' circulated. Men squeezed into seats and pulled the belts tight across their bellies and sat waiting, very erect, watching small clouds flash past. They sat and twenty minutes went by before the solid clunk of the lowered wheels was felt and finally the thump, bump, bump of the pilot doing a professional job of slamming the aircraft down on the brown land.

The engines' scream approached the pain threshold and the wing flaps slid out and down and the plane slowed from express train speed to a slow roll. The plane turned, pointing back along the gravel strip and traveled back through clouds and grayness, finally coming to a full stop in absolute silence.

The co-pilot sidled around the mound of freight, giving the boys an apologetic look as he made his way to the door-locking mechanism, where, with some help from the stewardess, he clanked, cranked and eventually swung the egg-shaped door open. The men piled out into the clear, clean air. In short order, baggage was offloaded and the men sorted it, searching the mound of bags, checking for a sleeping bag, hunting a flight bag. All the bags looked alike but the old hands had a routine. Nothing fancy. Two name tags, sometimes three, on the same hard-used green duffel bag and their Gladstone bag would have ROMA travel stickers or FLY JAL decals. Their bags were the first to be found and the first on the blue bus.

A battered bus with a Canadian Air Force stencil still on the door. The small Inuit driver had a big grin for everyone or an occasional 'Hi, how you?' for the guys returning from R and R. The door slammed shut and the bus took off up the gravel road. The luggage had been piled onto the seats and the men stood swaying, legs braced, a two-handed grip on the overhead rail.

Ken Ooglick, a would-be Daytona flat track contender, had been practicing and now double-clutched, shifting gears with barely a click-click. The old hands, who had in the past witnessed Ken grinding new gears from old, cheered and clapped, and Ken, proud of this new skill, waved off the applause.

The gravel road was a straight line from airport to the DEW-line site buildings. The landscape was stark: a black and white picture with an occasional splash of mottled dark-green lichen-encrusted flat rock. The men braced and swayed, affecting an indifference to the bleak land. The three miles of gravel were nothing and in four minutes the bus wheeled in to the parking area of Cam Main.

Chapter Five

The blue bus had been driven away, the mounds of luggage carried inside and Aaron, who had been at the tail of the line, took time to study his new mailing address. The men had offloaded in an area between two six-hundred-feet-long parallel buildings, connected in the center by a pedestrian bridge – thirty feet above Aaron's head – a large 'H' configuration.

What the American military had needed was a radio system, immune to atmospheric phenomena, that would connect northern radar consoles to the command center at Colorado Springs. The Canadian Arctic is a communication no-man's-land due to violent storms and magnetic disturbances. A solution was arrived at in the Massachusetts Institute of Technology (MIT) Lincoln labs where the Massachusetts scientists developed a radio that would work in these adverse conditions and called it a Forward Propagation Tropospheric Scatter system, or 'Troppo-Scatter' for short.

What also grew from the brain-storming sessions was a modular habitat, approximately four hundred feet in length, composed of units, each sixteen feet by twenty-eight feet joined at four-unit intervals, with accordion-pleated material making it into a weather-tight train. Covered with aluminum siding and with windows spaced at every eight feet, the extraterrestrial caterpillar chrysalis sat on stilts, three feet in the air. Towering above the aluminum-sided train, poised like a super giant golf ball on top of a sixty-foot tee, sat a faded white sphere, the Rae-dome. The white sphere was a protective shell encasing the constantly rotating radar antenna. The dome was huge, three hundred and sixty panels, each two feet by five feet, and in comparison, the buildings below were like so many packing crates laid end to end.

The antenna proper was steel and aluminum, being eighty feet long, thirty feet high and mounted on a steel plate, revolving three times a minute. At the control console below, the operator controlled this slow-turning top, moving the vertical inclination up or down within a twenty-degree arc or cranking the speed around from full stop to a rumbling five revolutions per minute. The drive motors, normally locked into an auto-servo system, could be switched to manual in emergency situations. The whole assembly weighed one hundred pounds more than twenty-seven tons.

The first 'Kabuna' (white man) to drop out of the sky arrived by ski plane under direction of J.D. Brannian, project surveyor, who hop-scotched the Arctic Circle staking ice strips for the landing of the United States Air Force (USAF) globe masters. Nuts, bolts and metal struts were delivered to a seven-thousand-strong workforce recruited from Canada, Australia, the USA, Asia and Europe. Inuit were recruited on site to assist in the assembly of the monster *Meccano* set. From the east and west coasts, cargo ships, preceded by the icebreaker, HMCS *Labrador*, brought two hundred thousand tons of material.

The senior man, Vern Bognall, the bell system engineer, had thirty-two months to be operational. Colorado Springs answered its first DEW-line telephone call in July of 1957, three months ahead of schedule.

Aaron knocked off the rubber-necking when he realized that he was alone in the parking area, whereupon he too climbed the stairs, entering the duchy of Cam Main through double-hung weather doors. A turn to the left, and ten feet along the hall, where he came to a three-feet-high counter that separated the common folk from the organized world of Carl Brewster.

Carl had retired from the regimented discipline of the Canadian Air Force and was still stiff-backed and upright, at parade rest; military from shiny shoes to shiny head. No wrinkles, no glasses and damned little hair; a tuft of white above each ear was all that remained after forty-two winters. It was thought that Carl had a good deal of money for he spoke knowingly of two-point dips, carried a margin account and could explain warrants and futures in detail. He was the office manager, the office being twenty by thirty feet, containing a long row of filing cabinets, Carl's polished desk, his clerk's not so polished desk and, on the end wall, Carl's addition to the world of efficiency, the Cam sector status board. The status board listed in alphabetical order all personnel assigned to the Cam sector and, if required, Carl updated the board hourly. He had arranged the board to indicate seniority, the man's trade, trade skills that needed upgrading and when, and the length of time left of the man's present contract. He could tell at a glance who was south, who was going south and which man might or might not return. Carl could assign new arrivals to work areas and beds without the fear of having two bodies being nose to nose for he strove for a no-conflict atmosphere. He kept the reservation clerk's power firmly grasped in his left hand whilst his right hand retained custody of the incoming mail.

The military dispatch pouch went directly to the station chief's office but personal mail was sorted and delivered by Carl. He had volunteered for this inferior duty even though to volunteer for anything was an anomaly normally found attendant with idiots or brown-nosers. He had been brought to the edge of madness when his weekly bottle of rye, securely packaged in six complete editions of the *Toronto Globe and Mail*, was violated by a very impudent junior clerk. This abomination had had the audacity to apply a ball-point hammer to Carl's package in what can only be rationalized as a demented state. Carl's *Globe and Mail* was still leaking when he retrieved it from his mailbox. He was in such a state that he indiscreetly volunteered for something: mail clerk duty.

When it was Aaron's turn at the counter, Carl gave him an open smile.

'Welcome to the land of the frozen dong. You must be Mrs. Dempster's little boy, Aaron.'

'That's me. The one and only.'

'Your room is halfway down the hall, Room 18. It's yours for six months or one hundred and seventy days. What the hell, let's round it out and call it a year.'

Carl detailed the cafeteria hours and explained that an Eskimo would clean the public areas but the bunk was his responsibility.

'You may want to swab the deck, hang some new art, turn the mattress, whatever. Help yourself to clean linen from the supply room. Any questions? By the way, there is an on-site rec committee called the North Triple S. They run the bar and distribute the libations.' Carl added, 'The bar will be open at 1700 hours. You will have a chance to meet the guys and have a beer before chow. If you have any problems, let me know.'

Aaron shook his head and asked, 'The North Triple S Club?'

'Right. The North of Seventy Shit Sifters.'

Aaron had been assigned Norm Bender's flop for he had gone south on that day's aircraft. He had been the supply supervisor and had furnished his private domain with the small extras that make life bearable, like wall-to-wall carpet, drapes, floor lamp, a walled-in closet. Aaron had lived with the military pecking order rule and these furnishings were going to need some explaining.

'Carl. Tell me it's my pretty blue eyes.'

'Problems already, Aaron?'

'No problem, but what's with the special treatment? That room is out of my league.'

'Let me clarify the situation, Aaron. The way things are, manpower wise, you are, or soon will be, the senior mux tech. As the main man, you will be asked to provide the morning market report and/or the morning Nevada odds, or you may be asked to secure a private phone line for you will be in charge of our communications with the south. The Shit Sifters appreciate the extra work entailed and this is the perk. Okay?'

'Wait up. What makes you so sure that I'll be lead hand? What about Crandell? He's more senior. I was told he has three years. What about him?'

'Crandell is senior but rest assured that this office does not err in the arrangement of sleeping quarters. In five weeks Crandell will be going out on year's end R and R and I know for a fact that he will be joining BC Tel. He won't be back.'

'It sounds great, in fact better than great but, Carl, what about experience? This is triple-A Carrier we're talking.'

Carl almost grinned.

'You have two months. The possession of the room will cause some motivation and we, the voting members of North of Seventy, will assist by any means available. We're counting on you. It won't be a big problem, Aaron, as the system is all in place.' Carl explained further. 'Crandell has cleared a circuit with Colorado Springs, installed a teletype and run, what he called "level and acceptance checks". He made some arrangement with Goose Bay for a private phone line and to date there has been no problem.'

'Sounds good.' Aaron thought for a moment and added, 'Sure, what the hell. I like the drapes.'

'Great, so go on down. Get settled in and introduce yourself at Room 20. Some of the charter members of the NTS are there and the bar will be open shortly. I'll catch you later.'

For the uninitiated, 'mux' is an abbreviation for 'multiplexing'. Multiplex is the generation of telephone equipment that replaced the thousands of wires that hung on the telephone poles that bordered every rural highway and byway coast to coast. With the use of crystal filters, it is possible to stack as many as twenty-four hundred phone users on one wire or a radio channel without an interfering signal between them. The nationwide telephone systems use this technique to transmit the millions of 'call someone you love' messages, the pages and pages of fax and the television extravaganzas that captivate the thinking audience. The big boys use it for networking and the military use it for the searching and saving of data, and on the odd occasion, a Montreal cardinal will receive a call to supply some Hastings Street go-go girl to the Vancouver Bayshore Inn. Nobody's perfect. The mux technology was a development of Lenkurt Electric of Palo Alto, California, an electronic research and development company, which, rumor had it, was subsidized with Pentagon petty cash.

Aaron had been at the Lenkurt test and calibration labs early in his electronic career and with one thing and another it gradually became industrial knowledge that he knew more than the average bear about multiplex. This was a major factor in Carl's 'Glad to meet you, these are the keys to the executive washroom' greeting. The senior Carrier tech, the man in charge of circuit orders, telephone lines, the PBX (Private Branch and Exchange), the mux, was the man to arrange direct communication with the south: the toll-free line to the broker, the banker and the candlestick maker.

The NTS club members respected Carl's intuition and intelligence regarding these matters; more importantly, Carl was the custodian of the Triple S Club's rolling bar. The original mandate of the club was not so much benevolent as protective. A drop of libation after a full shift of doing technical things is a civilized gesture but occasionally the party that developed would keep people awake. These people would go to work cranky or they'd yell abusive things at their next-door neighbors about keeping the noise down and other equally nasty remarks. The solution was to move the party and that was what the Triple S Club's rolling bar accomplished. The bar was moved to an area where it could best be utilized by those who would most enjoy it, without infringing on a co-worker's desire for peace and quiet. Any member who, through misjudgment, became unsavory or drunk or incoherent would be cautioned be Carl. A reprimand was usually a sufficient deterrent, but if the miscreant's rowdiness persisted, it was Carl's prerogative to advise the general membership, and that lesser person would suffer the 'barred from the bar' punishment for a week.

Aaron hung up his flight bag and made the bed but, being new boy on the block, delayed joining the gathering in Room 20. When Doc, Jake and Michael, who had been assigned beds in the transient rooms, wandered in, they were suitably impressed by the executive accommodation and soon the four greenhorns were making introductions to the assembled gathering of the Triple S members.

Several of the men present knew of Aaron and the monster overflowing a chair next to the bar was one of these.

'How are you, Aaron? I'm Noah. We're neighbors. I'm in Room 17. Help yourself to the poison,' he said.

With the formalities out of the way, he stuck out an enormous right hand for shaking. On the top of his head was a World War II brush cut and his black eyebrows were an almost solid line above brown, concerned eyes. A great hooked nose stuck out over the easy smiling mouth, and below the thirty pounds of head, there were what looked like two hundred pounds of muscled shoulders, chest and arms.

'How are you, Doc? You're Jake, right? How are you keeping? Good to see you, Michael. You boys have a good trip coming in? Ain't that mother a lot of fun?'

When the introductions around the room were complete and the company had drinks in hand, the working rules were laid out. The bar operated on the honor system; seventy-five cents an ounce and no tabs over twenty bucks. Members were free to open and use the bar at any time except for the eight hours before they were to go on shift, for the air force observer person was very sticky about sobriety at the radar console. It was a place to relax and have some small pleasures. So have you heard any good ones?

A stocky guy wearing a baseball cap picked up on that with, 'Did you hear that Jesus was Irish? Ya, that's right. They have proof that Jesus was Irish,' and with that start of the story, the party took on a more convivial nature.

Aaron was still thinking about the terms of his new lease, and he brought the subject up with Noah.

'What do you think about my getting Room 18? I don't want to be getting out of line.'

'It's no problem,' Noah replied. 'That is if you keep it. It has its drawbacks.'

'Carl told me the lead Carrier tech earns that kind of luxury.'

'Well, Aaron, that's partly right, but it's partly that no one else here would take it.'

'You're kidding.' Aaron frowned. 'Why the hell not?'

'Because of the next-door neighbor, Syd, Syd "fly-me-home" Smith.' Noah sipped some of his whisky and said, 'Syd is a little different. We, or at least I, think his plan is to fly himself south in an Ultralite that he's building from a kit. You know, a model airplane, only bigger, like full size. No rubber band wind-up propeller.'

The talk in the room had stopped. Noah poured some whisky into the bottom of his glass. Mac looked at Aaron and shrugged his shoulders. Someone popped a beer can and everybody settled back to listen.

Noah said, 'It's a fact... almost. He's worked up a flight plan, spotted and mapped some abandoned fuel dumps, drums of Av gas that have been left by oil company seismic crews all over the north, government weather stations and some of the mid-Canada sites that have been closed down. Syd has them all spotted.' He was silent for a moment, nodding his head. 'It's a long way south.'

'Is this guy serious?'

'Ya, the way it is, is that Syd has been here for eleven months on extended tour and when he got back from his last R and R, he worked out what his vacation had cost. That's when he swore he was here till he piled up ten grand. Well, he's been in eleven months and he gets a little more strange every day. He's a radician and a damn good tech but different. He'll drop in when the shifts change.'

Noah leaned back in his chair.

'So Aaron, I hear you were on that job in Turkey. How was it?'

'I only stayed three months. The money was no hell and them Turks are some mean mothers. How is Syd strange?'

'Fill him in, Al,' Noah gestured to a short fair guy in the corner. 'You've worked with Syd longer than anyone else.'

Al finished his drink and picked up the narrative.

'About six, maybe seven months ago, Syd sent south for a kit. At some stage, everybody builds a kit up here but Syd's was a bit more than most. He convinced the station chief that it was a delicate instrument and that he would have to assemble it in the dry air of his room.' Al continued, 'Johnson was station chief then, and he was about ready to head south, so it was no skin off his ass and he agreed. It was later, after Johnson had gone south, Davis was promoted to station chief and he figured that Syd had the job about wrapped up and so he let it go ahead. Davis and Syd split a bottle of Southern Comfort and Syd promised Davis he wouldn't build another Ultralite.'

Jake pointed across the hall to Room 16. 'He's building an Ultralite in there?'

'He is,' Al said. 'The frame, the wing, the engine, the whole ball of wax.'

'How big *is* room sixteen?' Jake asked.

'All the rooms are the same,' Noah explained. 'American Air Force regs are very exact about the contracted employee's bed size.'

'An Ultralite wouldn't fit.' This was from a skeptical Aaron.

'Take a look.' Noah waved his arm towards Room 16. 'Syd checked the measurements before he sent for the kit.'

The four new arrivals crowded in to what was left of the living space in Room 16. The room was still the regulation size quarters, but Room 16 was now a combined bed-sitting room-cum-machine shop. From a corner ceiling, above the window and down through the center of the room to the opposite floor corner, two aluminum structures were wedged. These structures were wing segments. From a large hook screwed into the ceiling, a pulley and chain supported what appeared to be an air-cooled engine block. On the floor below the engine, a large square tin pan was in place to catch any drips.

Along the back wall, a south-bend lathe had been installed and hanging on the wall above it were the chucks, clamps, cutting tools and the accessories of the home handyman's machine shop. The wall above the bed was adorned with a multitude of wrenches, calipers and various types of files and hammers. One corner had been lined with asbestos and had been used as a welding area. Room 16 was a neat, squeaky clean machine shop, tools all in place and not enough room left to swing a cat.

The boys looked and then returned to the bar for refills and answers.

'You look impressed,' Noah grinned. 'Bet you won't find that in a Howard Johnsons'.'

'That's for sure, but why the machine shop to assemble a kit?'

Al answered that one.

'Like we said, he plans to fly himself south. When he figured out the distance he could fly with the gas he would carry, he realized that he would need more gas to make it between fuel dumps, so now he is making some weight modifications to the original design.'

'Is he nuts?'

Noah smiled. 'He might be getting close.'

The general opinion was that Syd was different.

'But then again,' Noah pointed out, 'Syd has reduced the original weight by ninety-eight pounds and that works out to fifteen gallons of gas. He thinks he'll get forty miles to the gallon. That's how nuts he is.'

Doc asked, 'How will he get it out of the room?'

Noah explained.

'Syd claims that these outside walls can be opened by removing half a dozen six-inch lag bolts. Says that he can do it in twenty minutes.'

'Is he going to do any testing?'

'When's he going to try it?'

Noah waved his big hand.

'One at a time. He's already tested it, the engine that is. Al, you were there?'

'Oh Christ, was I? Jeez, the racket. It was two months ago and along with Syd's engine we had a roaring blizzard. It was blowing like hell outside and in here we had a four-cylinder engine running with no muffler. I thought there was a truck coming through the walls... and the smoke!'

Al laughed.

'Syd had his window open and then his door and the smoke poured out into the hall and he didn't catch the worst of it. The engine ran for what seemed like an hour and the whole damned building filled up with smoke—'

Noah butted in with, 'It was five minutes.'

'Ya, whatever. Anyway, the fire marshal called the console and the radician on duty pulled the emergency evacuation siren. Wait till you hear that thing. Anyway, it finally woke Davis, you know, the station chief?'

'We're supposed to meet him tomorrow.'

'Right. So anyway, Davis gets real hard with Syd. No more engine testing in the dorms.'

Noah, who had been sitting listening, added his remembrances to the story. He'd been the radician on console and had the honor of pulling the siren.

'No big deal, except that we could hear the engine noise at the console a quarter of a mile away. I couldn't figure out what the hell was going on.' Noah laughed and continued, 'Davis came running in, yelling his head off about an air raid, him still wearing the ear plugs he uses when he's sacked out.'

At 1800 hours, three new faces arrived at the door to Room 20, seats were rearranged, introductions completed and conversations resumed.

A stocky guy wearing a baseball cap was explaining the Irish joke. 'Jesus, Jesus Christ. It is being suggested in some ecclesiastical circles that he was Irish. Really, look at the known facts. The guy was still living at home when he was twenty-eight.'

Noah added, 'And he spent all his free time with buddies on the road. Right?'

'Yep, you heard it before?'

'A dozen times last night.'

Aaron found himself sitting next to a skinny six-foot, red-haired Ichabod Crane type.

'Aaron, hi. I'm Syd Smith. I hear you're my neighbor.'

'Syd, how are you? Noah was telling me about your Ultralite and, I confess, I went and looked it over and I tell you, I'm impressed. That's some surprise.' Aaron continued, ' So tell me, I've heard these small planes are very tricky.'

'Hard to fly and dangerous,' Syd replied. 'They're sensitive and they glide like a rock. I expect lift will require more power than the book suggests. Listen, drop in anytime; as a matter of fact I often need a third hand so if you hear me bang on the wall…'

'You bet, bang anytime. Noah thinks you might be using it for some fairly long trips.'

Syd looked away from Aaron before answering.

'I have given some thought to performance, mostly conjectural but soon, really soon, we will have the preliminaries out of the way.'

Syd was not the typical fighter pilot: old-fashioned, round glasses sat on the end of a pointy nose and below the nose, thin lips, a receding chin and an Adam's apple that bobbed up and down. He finished his drink and busied himself building another.

'How about you, Aaron? Ready for another?'

'Not yet. How long will it be before you fly it?'

'She's ready now. I've been cleaning up some loose ends and the weather hasn't been that great. I need some relative calm or at least no winds over ten miles an hour.' Syd continued, 'I wouldn't want any unexpected happening. I noticed last year that when we got into the twenty-four-hour daylight the weather was superb, and strangely that's when the Inuit have the best fish catches. It's warm, around sixty, and if you can believe it, this is almost a great place to be.'

And then, Aaron brought up the subject of noisy neighbors.

'Jeez, Aaron, two months ago, I got carried away, forgot the time, but I always tried to work the noise in when the guys in the rooms around mine were on shift. There's been the odd small incident… like when the assembly slipped on the hoist one night, around 2:00 A.M. and the prop went through the wall into Room 18. But the damn walls are only quarter-inch plywood. What the hell! The blade was more like two feet than two inches from Norm's head. Jeez! He was supposed to be working. The way some guys go on.' He shook his head. 'Do I look like I would kill someone? Anyway, the rough work is finished. Nothing left now but some polishing, that kind of thing.'

The stocky guy was explaining about Jesus once again.

'He *was* Irish. Look, he never married, spent most of his adult life with the boys and if you listened to his mother he was a saint amongst men, and that's not all...'

The remainder of the story was lost in general conversation, the clink, buzz and loud social grouping of men determined on relaxing.

In the morning the four new arrivals met with the station chief, Jack Davis, and were assigned their work locations, the hutch they would call home for the next six months. Michael and Doc were assigned positions at eastern Auxiliary fun sites called Cam One and Cam Three. Jake was to make his way westward to the adjacent Auxiliary site of Pin Four. The eastern plane was leaving in forty-five minutes and the western bird was scheduled for departure twenty minutes later and Mr. Davis strongly recommended that the men be aboard at the time of take-off.

Aaron drew the best hand. He was assigned main site duty, exactly as George had predicted. The four greenhorns would keep in touch by way of the site service channel, a phone connection between all sites, much like a rural phone line.

In the next month Aaron settled in, working up to the swing of things. Finding his way around. He sent south for a model boat kit, spent several evenings sorting out the bumps on the rec-room pool table and spent a lot of time with Syd, polishing, painting and policing the *South Bound Adventurer*; the name had been supplied by Aaron. Big Noah was another active participant for, with his bulk, he could substitute as a forklift on occasions. Wednesday, during the second week in July, the three men – Syd, Noah and Aaron – finished the 3:00 P.M. to midnight shift and headed straight for Room 16. Noah had stopped for a bottle of rye and was the last to arrive. With a down-the-hatch, mud-in-your-eye ritual drink but no other waste of time, they began stripping the quarter-inch plywood off the outside wall, exposing the pink insulation and the eight six-inch lag bolts. The wall construction was exactly as Syd had said and in twenty minutes, with Noah on one side and Aaron and Syd grunting on the other, they lowered the outside wall to the spongy lichen-covered tundra, the *Playboy* centerfolds still Scotch-taped in profusion, window still intact. Another ten minutes of pushing and grunting and yells of 'Easy, easy', and the wing segments were stretched out beside the resting wall. They took a break and passed the bottle around.

One hour later, the Ultralite sat assembled, engine bolted in place, propeller mounted, wing secured, basket seat centered between the tubular frame members and, above, blessed by the Norse God, Boreas, the cloud-free blue sky completed the euphoria. Before the wall was restored to its proper function, Noah passed out two club chairs, and there Aaron and Noah sat, having a drink or two or six.

The red sun ball was heading up and away from the horizon and the green moss and the Arctic flowers were framed by the blue sea and blue sky and Syd and his machine filled up the center of a once-in-a-lifetime picture. Occasionally, Syd asked for a screwdriver, a wrench, or a drink, but other than minor interruptions the helpers sat and eyeballed the horizon-to-horizon, giant, 2:00 A.M. Arctic outdoor morning. At the bottom of the bottle, Syd joined them.

'All done.' He drained the last drops. 'All ready.'

'Fire and fly time?' Noah asked.

Syd muttered something like, 'Right on, fire and fly time.'

Aaron took a long look at Syd, for his last remark had definitely been nervous.

'You okay, Syd? We could do this tomorrow!'

'I'm fine. The bird's fine and shit, man, this is it. No sweat in the Arctic, right?'

Syd climbed into the basket seat and started the engine. A cloud of blue-black smoke hung over the shiny machine and the air was filled with the power sound of a smooth-running, four-cylinder, air-cooled engine and the distinctive throb of it became a life rhythm. An alien thing in this land of icebergs. Syd tightened the seat belt, pulled out the throttle, left hand wrapped around the funny-shaped joystick, right hand on throttle, head encased in a white helmet, his half-open blue-gray parka flapping in the wind stream. Then slowly, slowly the machine began to roll and the whole assembly tilted forward and leveled out and Syd grinned a faceful of teeth-grin and then the machine was up, bee-buzzing in pursuit of the horizon.

Noah grabbed Aaron and they danced a small jig and looked again and the Ultralite was eighty feet off the ground, level with the aircraft beacon antennas and moving away from the site. Without saying a word, Noah ran back into the dorm and Aaron headed for the garage. In a very short time, Aaron roared up to the main entrance, driving the station chief's half-ton truck. Noah burst through the door with a new bottle in hand but when they got to the landing strip there was nothing but the empty blue sky. No Ultralite.

Aaron stopped the truck and they got out and stood looking. Noah tossed the bottle top towards the hangar and passed the bottle to Aaron. Aaron didn't take his eye from the horizon.

Noah said, 'There're a couple of other guys who're going to want some of that.'

About then, the throb of an air-cooled, four-cylinder engine could be heard coming from the beach and there, just off the ground, was the *South Bound Adventurer*. The Ultralite rolled to a stop in front of the truck and Syd turned the engine off and sat in the funny wire seat and grinned and grinned. The three shook hands and rubbed heads and passed the bottle around.

Syd clasped their hands and said, 'Thanks.'

At 1600 hours, the weekly DC-4 Winnipeg flight, number 196, had finished the turnaround. Noah and Aaron had helped Syd and the two Inuit baggage handlers load and tie down three crates that held the *South Bound Adventurer*.

Noah said something to Syd about, 'Send us a card,' and Syd assured him that he would.

Aaron was still puzzled. 'You never were going to fly her south?'

'I'm not crazy, Aaron.'

'So why the game?'

'When the rumor started, I denied it and denied it but no one wanted to believe me. It was January and every guy on the site was consciously or unconsciously wanting to go south. They used the Ultralite, aggrandized it, even the skeptics, and everybody working out the best route. The miles between the fuel dumps, the weather and everybody on the site was involved. Something to do.'

'What about the equipment, the lathe, the welding?'

'Stage dressing and I needed something to pass the time.' Syd continued, 'Noah, will you crate up the tools and send them out with the August sea-lift?'

'You got it.'

And then the DC-4 was gone… south.

Chapter Six

At two o'clock in the morning, Michael pushed his chair away from the games-room table. He swore softly and then swore again, and then he smashed the tabletop with a clenched fist, which made the stout, round tabletop bounce, causing ripples and openings in the multicolored jigsaw puzzle assembled in the center of it. The brilliant reds, oranges, yellows and vivid blues merged into a desert scene featuring a large spiked cactus predominantly in the foreground with brown and blue sky merging into the background. There were five glaring holes, five pieces missing, five points of emptiness and once again Michael swore.

'That lousy son of a bitch! That half-witted bastard! He's known all week that there were five pieces missing. Laughing, no wonder he's been laughing. That smart-assed bastard! Okay, dickhead, we'll see about that,' and, disregarding the lateness of the hour, Michael stormed out of the room and through the darkened hallway to the Cam-One 'J' mechanic's room.

The sudden banging of the door alerted the sleeping man's unconscious mechanism, and he was half-sitting up in the bed when Michael switched on the bright overhead light.

'What is it? What the hell do you want?'

Henri Bechet was a small, fat, black-haired, black-eyed, normally tidy individual, but on this occasion Michael found him somewhat rumpled. The sleep-puffed eyes glanced quickly towards the loud, ticking alarm clock.

'It's two thirty. What the hell are you doing? What do you want?'

'You know damn well what I want. I want the five pieces of that puzzle, you simple-minded jerk. You think this is some kind of a joke? You've been laughing all week. Well, now I'll give you something to laugh about, like a kick in the ass. I want the five pieces to that puzzle, asshole, or I'm going to start making—'

Michael's voice stopped abruptly as he was firmly gripped from behind, and wrapped up and wheeled around back into the hallway by Harry Edwards, the large, muscular station chief. With one arm wrapped around Michael, Harry reached back into the room and switched off the light.

'Go back to sleep, Henri, just go back to sleep. I'll take care of this.'

He shut the door, then, whilst still retaining Michael's arm in a convincing hammerlock, the two quick-marched the length of the hallway to the station office where Michael was brusquely deposited onto a straight-back wooden chair.

'Now, you just sit there, mister. Sit there and don't say a damn word. I've every reason to ship you south. I should, first thing tomorrow, and I should send that Frenchman with you. This is crap, Michael. The two of you, acting like a couple of kids. This high-school grab-ass is going to stop.'

Michael opened his mouth to speak but the station chief held up a hand.

'No, you cool down. I don't want to hear it yet.'

Michael sat, the redness of his face slowly receding, his breathing returning to normal and almost reluctantly he relaxed. After several minutes he fumbled in a shirt pocket and pulled out cigarettes.

'I'm sorry, Harry. It was too much. I'm sorry.'

'What the hell was it all about? I heard you up here and I was asleep.'

The station chief used the connecting room for living quarters and Michael could see the rumpled bed beyond the open door.

'It's the puzzle, the one Henri was working on last week. A picture of the desert that he spent four days on. Fifteen hundred pieces and he wouldn't let anyone near it and when he had finished it he broke it all up and said if we wanted to see it, we would have to be as smart as him. Well, the son of a bitch kept out five pieces.'

'For Christ's sake, Michael – five pieces. What makes that a crime? Maybe they're on the floor or they may not have been there to start with. You may have lost them yourself.'

'Aw hell, Harry, I looked. I looked everywhere. Down on my hands and knees, and besides… well, every time Henri went by the rec room, ever since I started the puzzle, he's been laughing and giggling and making remarks like, "We'll see, smart guy." He's driving me nuts. I'll soon be as crazy as him. He's crazy, Harry.'

'You think you're sane right now? Storming down there, into his room? You owe him an apology and first thing tomorrow, no, I mean this morning, you'll do it or by God, Michael, you're going south.'

Henri had not gone back to sleep. He lay, staring at the blackness, listening to the station generators. The throbbing engines were like the voices of old friends. Tonight, two plants were in use, and they were having a small argument, a slight difference about who would lead and who would follow. Silly engines, you must work together. But the engines disregarded Henri's thoughts and continued broadcasting the slight dissonance.

Like the men here, Henri thought. Not together, not helping. If it weren't for my abilities, they would freeze, with no lights, no heat and no radar. So who cares? Instead, the damned redhead and his smart-ass remarks. Damn these English. Always the putdown at meals: how to hold a fork; here, try some ketchup on that porridge. And the cooks are just as bad. No food served to greasy coveralls. Christ, as if I had time to change clothes every time I have to piss. Who the hell are they anyway? These guys? I've been an apprentice, done my time. I'm as much a technician as those electronic types. Henri continued to brood about the imagined injustice. Let them run the diesels. Christ, the lights would be out in an hour. Sure, put them in the powerhouse for a day.

At six thirty, Harry knocked on Henri's door. He knocked several times and when he received no reply, he pushed it open and went in. Henri, fully dressed, was sitting on the room's only chair, staring through the opaque, frost-covered window. The bed was stripped, the bedding folded and stacked on the striped mattress and in front of the naked closet were two packed suitcases.

'Are you moving somewhere?' Harry stood in the doorway, ignored by Henri. 'Henri… Henri?'

The silence in the room was pervasive and the man in the chair remained still. Harry stood for another minute and then sat down on the bare mattress.

'About last night… Michael is sorry, damned sorry. He'll be coming by to apologize.'

43

The apology was rejected, the monologue ignored, indeed Henri had yet to glance at the station chief, but sat staring at the blank window, and shortly Harry stood up.

'Look,' he said, 'I know you're sore. Okay, but come down to the office after awhile. I'll find a bottle and we can talk it over. Okay?'

The station chief was still in the doorway when Henri did speak. 'I quit.'

'I can see that, but how about waiting until I get a replacement?'

'I quit, as of now, Harry.'

'Well, if that's how you feel, but there's no plane... nothing for four days. Could be five days... a week... so how about putting in time until a plane comes in?'

'I quit today, Harry. To hell with this place and to hell with the job and to hell with the men. I quit. I'll go home now. Please.'

'Go home? Christ, nobody's going anywhere till the weather clears and that might be another week.'

Again Henri said, 'I quit.'

Harry could invoke no further response. Henri remained in his room until the 2100 hours coffee break when he went to the dining room, ate two sandwiches, had some coffee and went back to his room without a word to anyone. The next morning Harry tried to reason with Henri again, but again, gave up in disgust and anger. Once more Henri appeared at the evening coffee break, feasted on two sandwiches and, still in silence, returned to his room.

At 3:00 A.M. the console operator called Harry to report an alarm from the generator room's outside exit. Roger, the tech on the midnight shift, had checked it out and secured the door and reported, 'No alarms, all normal. Incidentally, Henri is not in his room. The guy must have gone out for a walk and left the door open.' Roger continued, 'He'll be back soon. There's forty degrees of frost out there and a thirty-knot wind.'

'Thanks,' Harry said. 'Call me when Henri shows up.'

Henri did not show up that night or the next for Henri was going home. He had traveled sixty-five miles across the ice when the right side flexible track of the Nodwell all-terrain vehicle broke loose from the front idler sprocket. Sixty-five miles was a remarkable achievement.

At 2300 hours, when the men of the site were preparing for bed,

Henri had carried his sleeping bag and two suitcases through the engine room, out of the back door and across the windblown roadway to the garage. He had checked the oil and topped up the gas tank of the all-terrain vehicle. He started it up and sat, listening, and when the engine was running smoothly and he had heard no strange squeaks or bangs he smiled in a strange manner, happy that this engine ran smoothly. He proceeded with checking the cab's heater, the roof-mounted spotlight and the under-the-seat first aid kit. Finding no faults, he shut the machine off whilst he returned to the dorms.

In the kitchen, he made six ham sandwiches and packed them along with apples, tins of fruit and tins of juice into an empty cardboard box. He saw no one whilst he was assembling his box lunch and he was back in his room and pulling on his bulky Arctic clothing before he heard anyone. It was Harry knocking at the door.

'Henri?'

Henri remained silent, and Harry knocked and called again.

'Henri?'

'Ya, what is it?'

'How are you feeling?'

'I'll be okay, Harry.'

'How about it, Henri? Do you want to talk?'

'No.'

Henri waited for half an hour after Harry's visit before he carried his box lunch out to the bombardier, raised the overhead door and drove directly away from the site into the windblown snow. He did not bother with lights until he had the machine aimed at the beach. When he did switch them on, they were of very little use, illuminating more snow than landscape.

The snow was drifting and forming into long curving ridges and the all-terrain vehicle behaved like a small row boat… bobbing up and over the wind-packed lanes of snow.

He had forgotten the pressure ridges of ice that piled up on the beach and it took two hours to find a path through the tons of broken, house-sized slabs. He eventually slid and drove through the litter to arrive at the flat table that was the frozen Arctic Ocean. He stopped and had a sandwich.

He clambered down out of the machine and checked his

direction against the brightest star in the southern sky. He didn't know the name of it but he had observed that it was the first and brightest star to appear above the southern horizon and for the last two months it had been directly over Cam Main before it faded in the morning.

The wind and blowing snow eased, and for the next three hours Henri made excellent time. Things began to sour at daybreak for, shortly after eight, the way west ended at a black ribbon of open water. The hundred-foot mutilation of ice ran from north to south as far as Henri could see. Henri turned north, and drove an extra hour before he found a point where the lead narrowed and he could cross. He had timed his detour and was so able to return to his original westward path.

The sun was high: a red ball of fire and the rays reflected off the white ice would blind. Henri did not appreciate that the unfiltered sunlight could be the cause of his death. He was wearing dark glasses but in a very brief time they fogged up and then he removed them until such time as they cleared. Eventually, he left them off entirely and within the hour, he was suffering a severe headache and his eyeballs felt like he had rubbed sand on them. Enough. Time now for a break; an escape from the bright glare. He sat with his head twisted away from the glare of the windshield, munching a sandwich and staring into the dark corners of what was becoming a motorized igloo. Even with the engine running, and the heater on full, Henri could see his breath and if the engine were to fail, the interior would soon embrace the minus-thirty-degree outside temperature.

The metal walls were painted a dark blue, in some areas splotched by white frost. Shafts of daylight filtered through three small cabin windows. Frost was layered all over the glass except for a small pie-shaped section in front of the driver and Henri kept his head turned away from that source of irritation. He finished the sandwich and dozed, but not for long.

Abruptly he straightened up and with red-rimmed eyes checked the engine gauges and then scrambled outside and stood urinating a yellow stream on the white ice. He stood leaning forwards, straining to see the horizon, paying no attention when the warm fluid splashed on his gloved hand. The yellow stream stopped and he arranged his fly, still scanning the distant skyline. Absentminded, he rubbed his eyes and yelped in pain when drops of urine made contact with his inflamed eye. Cursing, and with tears streaming down his face, he clambered back into the machine. Very cautiously, he touched his fingers to his eyes, testing the swelling and then shaking his head. The pain! Oh God, spare me this pain!

Squinting, blinking, head cocked to one side, straining to see and finally, with his head almost touching the windshield, he revved up the engine and started the machine lurching forward. The solidly built bombardier lurched and jerked an erratic half a mile and gave up. The abrupt changes of direction were too much and the right-hand track peeled over and off the forward idler sprocket with a banging clatter.

Henri sat for a long minute and then cursed and pounded both fists on the front panel.

'You bastard! You filthy bastard!'

He knew, he knew only too well what had happened. He had serviced this machine a month earlier and found the same problem, and he knew that here and now the repair was impossible. He sat, his mind searching for an escape. Christ, will those bastards laugh. Well, up theirs. I'll walk. By morning my eyes will be okay, and I'll walk. Can't be more than ten miles, well, maybe fifteen, but so what. If I keep moving I'll be warm. A sleep and then a brisk walk to Cambridge Bay and there'll be a DC-4 waiting to take me home.

Harry checked Henri's room before breakfast. When he realized the man had gone he assigned two men to search the site.

'Check the warehouse and the hangar and while you're at it, take a look in the emergency shelter and when you find him... oh hell, I don't know. See if he'll buy the idea of a plane coming in.'

At 0900 hours the searchers were back, but without Henri.

'Not in any building on the site,' they reported. 'He might be wandering around down on the airstrip, but with a forty-knot wind blowing, we can't see spit out there.'

Harry asked them to look again. 'And check the vehicles, the track vehicles...'

Fifteen minutes later, Harry called the main site to report a man missing. 'Maybe headed across the ice. We've got a bombardier missing from the truck garage.'

Harry asked Stephen Kanatuk to come in and help. Stephen was a part-time Inuit employee. He was twenty-two, single and spent the days trapping fox, chasing Lucy Planaka or working for Federal Electric. Harry explained the situation.

'An air search is out of the question until the wind drops and that might be three or four days.'

'Two days,' Stephen said. 'Two days and then very cold.'

'You may be right, Steve, but that man won't last two days out on the ice and his chances of finding Cambridge Bay are damned near zero, so you're on the payroll. As soon as you're ready, head out for Cambridge Bay. You might find him somewhere between here and there. Do you need anything?'

'I'll be okay. I'll take my snow mobile. I know it's in good shape and I can go now. I could use some gas.'

'Who are you taking with you?'

The Inuit shook his head and Harry said, 'Hey now, you can't go alone. Another man and a radio and another snow mobile just in case, if something happens you have a backup. Two of you in case of trouble. No argument, and I know just the volunteer.'

Michael arrived at the office and after the situation had been explained to him, his instantaneous response was to grin and to say, 'What are we waiting for?' Michael's feelings were mixed. He thought the 'J' mechanic was a jerk and having watched Henri's performance for the past week, Michael had decided that the man was a certifiable idiot. It didn't occur to Michael that he was in some way responsible for Henri's insane journey. Enough of these pompous 'J' mechanics; now we'll have some adventure.

They were on the trail by ten o'clock. There was thirty degrees of frost but the wind had abated and the sun was high. The blue sky was a pastel dome, separated from the white land mass by a black pencil line at the horizon. When they reached the high point of the trail, the ocean ice pressure ridge, Michael produced a pair of ten-power binoculars and scanned the stark landscape. Stephen cautioned him about the prolonged use of the high-powered binoculars.

'You get reflections off the surface and damn quick you're snow blind.'

They made good time but at 1300 hours the level trail ended at a fault in the sea ice; thirty yards of open water. The black water, like an obscene ink blob on a white linen tablecloth, stretched north and south as far as the eye could see.

'Damn it, Steve, we've passed him. We'll have to backtrack.'

'Maybe not. First, we take tea-time, then I think we better go along there,' said Stephen, waving a gloved hand north. 'This ice opened after the wind went down. The tide changed, the ice cracked. The old ones explained that the small ice always chased the sun and the strong ice stayed home. We can go around. We'll head north and in a few miles we can be on the other side. Take a little longer, but we'll be okay.'

'You're sure?'

'Damned sure. You bet.'

Stephen busied himself with a primus stove, preparing for tea-up. Michael searched the Big Empty with the binoculars.

'That maniac could have driven right into the ocean. This is a waste of time, Steve.'

Stephen paused in his preparations, and then standing, he shaded his eyes. A moment later he pointed.

'Over there, Mike. See? Move the glasses down, right about there.'

The yellow and black machine sat, a door hanging open, with no movement and no smoke from the exhaust. Henri's arctic sled was now a dead thing, as frozen as the surrounding landscape. Michael spent a minute observing, searching the arranged still life on snow for details.

'It looks like he threw a track. Here, take a look.'

'Right on, Mike. That's what happened, and I think he started walking. We can go damned quick and be over there before night.'

The direct distance between Cam One and Cam Main is eighty-six miles. The Cam One site was built on Jenny Lind Island and Cam Main was built on Victoria Island. When Henri left the warmth and comfort of Cam One to cross that part of the Arctic Ocean, the ocean was not so much ocean as it was ice, acres of ice. Ice in sheets, ice in cubes, ice in blocks, ice in every shape and size conceivable, great chunks of ice piled in to ridges fifty foot high. These pressure ridges are the result of sea ice piling up on the shore and as the ocean continues to freeze, more pan ice piles up on the immovable clutter deposited earlier. The frozen acres between the pressure ridges are not stationary. All in all, it is no place for a golf course.

There is a continuous eastern movement and in all movements of large masses, faults develop, cracks in the surface that can widen into mile-wide fissures of open, black water and a day later close up, leaving no trace of the imperfection. Such was the fault that had forced Henri, Michael and Stephen on a twelve-mile detour.

Before beginning the open water detour, Michael made a determined effort to advise Cam Main of the situation. The bulky UHF (ultra high frequency) radio was limited to distances not exceeding thirty miles, and Cam Main being forty miles away was not even a hope. The man hunters wasted no further time, but it was the sun's twilight that shone on them as they pulled up beside the abandoned snow machine.

The machine was empty. No Henri and no indication of when he had left or where he had gone. The patches of windblown snow held no footprints, no sign of human passage. Michael tried Cam Main again but shortly gave up in disgust.

'We'll have to get closer to Cambridge Bay for this thing to work, Steve. If we could talk to them, they could get a plane up. He must be out there between us and now that the weather has cleared, they could find him a lot faster from the air.'

'Not tonight, Michael.'

'No, they can't search at night.'

'Okay, Michael. We stay here. We could pass him in the dark and if we travel at night we must go very slow. We can start very early and be sure we see him.'

'Sure, but what if he's hurt?'

'We can't help him at night, Michael.'

'Okay, we'll stay here. We could pass him in the dark, or even drive right over the silly bastard. That would make a great accident report. "The lost man, run over by rescuers."'

'Ya, more better we stay here.'

The rescue team slept very little and by 5:00 A.M. they were up, drinking coffee and planning the day. It was agreed that Stephen would follow in Henri's tracks whilst Michael headed for a distant ridge. They would join up again as soon as Michael had examined the distant terrain with the powerful binoculars. Further action would be decided by what was found. Half an hour later, Michael crested the ridge and at the same time his radio crackled into life.

'Michael Clow here.'

'Michael. Cam Main here. We have some news for you.'

At 0800 hours, Michael and Stephen were sitting in the Cam Main dining room enjoying hot coffee and hearing the conclusion of Henri's odyssey.

The previous day, an hour before the rescuers had sighted the abandoned tracked vehicle, a party of five seal hunters had stumbled into Henri's snow and sun retreat. Henri was snow-blind. The Inuit spoke very little English and Henri knew even less Inuit but conversation was not required. The hunters rearranged the load of seals and in quick time they headed out for Cambridge Bay. The Inuit, skidoos, toboggans, seals and Henri. They were disposed to leaving him at the white person's hospital, but Henri would have none of that.

Henri was reduced to standing beside the toboggan, yelling, 'Airport, airport, take me to the airport.'

Standing in the middle of the track into town, snow-blind, flapping his arms, mouthing childlike sounds of an airplane's engine, Henri convinced the Inuit they should consult with a higher authority. They went to find the priest.

The priest, a native of Montpellier in France, and having only recently arrived in Canada, found Henri's provincial dialect as difficult to interpret as the Inuit had. He sent for a Mountie and the Mountie, being a practical person, bundled Henri off to the hospital. The Mountie had established that Henri had not been abandoned by a Russian submarine. The Mountie further swore that there were no foreign vessels in Canadian waters and that, also, Henri was a Federal Electric employee. When the Cam sector superintendent was advised, he hummed and hawed and then dealt with the matter in a logical manner. He arranged for Henri's immediate departure south. The first plane south after the storm was at seven thirty. Henri was on it.

At 0800 hours, the DC-4 climbed away from Cambridge Bay

heading south, and Henri, eyes swathed in white bandages, smiled and smiled.

'Showed those assholes, sure did.'

The stewardess, passing in the aisle, stopped at his side. 'Pardon, sir?'

'Nothing, nothing, just talking to myself. I've been in a damned long time. Too long.'

Michael found a large plain envelope in his weekly mail. It was the first thing he opened and the enclosed brochure, printed in five colors, advertised a new Winnipeg business. Highlighted were survival kits designed for sportsmen who were going to the high Arctic and the enterprise was owned and operated by Henri Bechet, a renowned Arctic traveler. A personal note to Michael suggested that Michael could purchase any item at cost plus ten. The note finished with a scrawled: *Call me anytime. Henri.*

Michael swore and swore again, but as he crumpled the envelope and brochure before dumping it in the wastebasket, some loose material in the envelope caught his attention. He shook the crumpled paper and five irregular-shaped pieces of a jigsaw puzzle fell into his hand.

Chapter Seven

The technicians in transit had endured a three-day layover at Cam Main, awaiting the arrival of the sector aircraft. The blue and white DC-3 had been busy with mail deliveries on the western leg of its scheduled route when it had encountered ice fog. It was thirty-six hours before the aircraft returned to the main site and the afternoon of her arrival was used for refueling and loading of cargo. The transit tech became a logistical problem bed-wise and meal-wise. They had been placed on hold in a frigid Quonset hut that had been designated as the airport VIP lounge, and they waited, wearing full Arctic issue of parka, flight pants and mukluks.

The *Arctic Rose*, their blue and white chariot, had been parked three hundred feet from the door, engines idling, props turning, and the waiting men momentarily expected the call to board. Nothing could be seen through the ice-covered windows; however, the muted roar of the aircraft engines was becoming a real mother-freaking headache in the otherwise quiet, square, drab room.

The wooden panel of the dispatch office window crashed up and the dispatcher's head demanded, 'What the hell do you guys want? The pilot's on board and ready to go. Move your asses.' The wooden panel crashed down.

The seven men were stopped at the boarding steps as the second officer checked names against the manifest and then, one by one, they filed up the steps and into the darkness of the plane.

Still fully clothed in their Arctic issue, they crammed themselves into the well-used flight seats. With no further formalities, the elliptical door clanged shut behind them and the second officer scuttled up the narrow aisle, past them into the dimly lit cockpit.

A variety of cardboard boxes, sacks of grocery items, miscellaneous steel drums, tractor and generator parts had been stacked around the men. To contain the rough, agglomerate mounds, large nets of canvas webbing had been fastened with snap hooks to steel rails sunk into the splintered plywood floor. Room for the seven seats had been left along the starboard bulkhead of the airborne moving van but the seating arrangement was not spacious.

There was the roar of both engines and a terrible rattling of the cargo settling, the floor vibrating, seats shaking and then, just before everything came loose, the brakes were released. The plane rolled away from the warmth of the dimly lit Quonset hut, into the frozen blackness.

Still muffled in parkas and flight pants, the seven sought solace from the noise and cold by pulling the parkas tighter and burrowing deeper into the seats. There was a relative quiet as the plane lifted off the snow-packed runway and all the hardware, boxes, bags and barrels settled up against a neighbor.

When the plane leveled off, several men stood, stretched and sought more comfort squatting on cargo and settling buttocks onto the elasticity of the cargo net. A deck of cards appeared and yet another game of Stuke was under way, using a mail sack as the table. Crates and mailbags were pressed into service for club car seating and the arrangements were finalized with five players. Nick, the cook, too drunk to undo his seatbelt was soon making snores and spitting bubbles. The seventh man, a greenhorn, was ignored.

Some things never change. The return from R and R is always a black period. A hangover, lost luggage or a 'Why the hell am I here?' time.

Going out; now going out is something else. Away to the neon rainbow with a fat wallet, and strutting into the land of booze with silky broads, sunshine, fresh milk, new cars and green grass. And now this… For another six months, this desolate place of frost and cold, six months of mind-numbing solitude.

The dealer had yet to be Stuked when the plane began descending. Without a word the men resumed the role of passengers, and squirming and twisting, they buckled up. The dissonant rattle, bang, bong, melody picked up and, with a good two-bump landing, the plane was on the ground and rolling towards a distant halo of light in the blowing snow.

The co-pilot appeared and scrambled towards the tail and one of the old hands yelled a warning in time to save his bare hand from making contact with the super-cold dogging mechanism of the cargo door. With the frost-covered door open, snow blew in, bringing

Tony Mack with it.

Tony was the Cam One station chief and he was there to take consignment of his cargo, which included Nick, the cook. Tony was not impressed with Nick's inability to speak and he growled something about needing hands to offload. The passengers' status was reviewed, the luxury class was deleted and Tony made six field promotions. The change in status was to be effective immediately. The boys became men. No exceptions. Wow! Promoted!

Cargo hands busily wrestled boxes and bags through the door to the idling half-ton truck ten feet below.

Nothing fragile in this bag, is there, boss?'

With a surly, 'Happy New Year,' Tony departed and the cargo door was muscled home, dogged down and the big bird made ready to fly another hundred miles. Rattle, bang, crash, up and away and then the quiet of flight; the muted roar of the engines, the whistle of an air leak at the cargo door.

Once again the men arranged the card game seating and they included the greenhorn who claimed he was in possession of some loose coin of the realm. The game, Jacks or better, was underway ten minutes after take-off. A small consolation was that the bulk of the cargo was destined for Cam Two; fifty sheets of four by eight plywood. When it was gone there would be plenty of room to stretch.

Cam Two had a hangar and a small problem. Manny Bitman, the station chief, had checked and found that the motor-driven doors were frozen in place. Normally the massive doors, equipped with flanged wheels rolling on a steel track, opened as slick as a knife going through butter but on that winter's eve, the door's steel track system was filled with ice. This was a nuisance but what the hell: 'We'll offload on the pad.' Manny would look at the doors in daylight or in the spring. Whatever.

The *Arctic Rose* taxied up the runway to the welcoming committee and parked on the wind-blown, snow-free apron beside the frozen doors. The area was well lit by a multitude of large arc lights. Wheel blocks were placed, the cargo door swung open and eight men began moving the four by eight-foot wooden sheets from the plane to the truck that was parked below the cargo door. Two men maneuvered a sheet through the door to the waiting hands of several hardy men who were balancing precariously on the sides of the truck. The men and lumber were promptly blown six feet onto the rock-hard apron. After a second team suffered a similar displacement by the prop wash, the pilot shut down the port engine. The pilot knew he would have trouble starting that engine in the minus forty-degree elements and he specified twenty minutes as a maximum limit on the downtime. The reason he agreed to any shutdown was that sheets of plywood were flying from the cargo door like big kites, and were crashing into the tail assembly before gaining altitude. With the propeller still, offloading was completed in quick order and well within the twenty minutes and they proceeded with start-up.

They were fifteen minutes late. The radial engine was frozen. Locked up. A no-go. The station chief was now forced to deal with the unpleasant task of opening the fifty-foot-high hangar doors. Air force regs are all-encompassing, thorough, emergency situation stuff, and Manny knew the regs.

With little preamble the station chief and one of the Inuit, Simon, drove to the POL (petroleum oil lubricants) storage area and loaded a forty-five-gallon drum of de-icer fluid. De-icer is an alcohol-based liquid stocked at all DEW-line sites for frozen hangar door situations. In no time at all, Manny, Simon and a couple of the temporary cargo hands, who were dragged out of the twenty-below comfort of the hangar, were slopping the almost raw alcohol along the length of the hangar doors. The results were dramatic. As soon as the stuff hit the frozen door track the ice began to crackle and dissolve and the powerful alcohol fumes soon had the work party laughing and almost enjoying the rough job. Manny quipped that for the next party he'd sell tickets. The three-phase overhead electric motors whined, the doors growled, something clanged and the huge doors rattled open. A tow bar was fastened to the DC-3's nose and the *Arctic Rose* came in from the cold. The super-quick hangar heaters did their job and soon water was running down the sides of the frozen bird, forming large muddy pools on the hangar floor. Some of the men wandered around the plane, kicking the tires and eventually the pilot started the engines, causing a lot of smoke and noise.

The hangar doors smoothly rolled aside and with no more fuss the 'New Year Special' was on her way to Cam Three with the dead-tired, now unemployed cargo hands, now too few in number to play any kind of card game.

At Cam Two, the airport detail joined the remnants of the New Year's Eve party. The Inuit, Simon and Old Tooth, continued on for another half a mile to the staff married quarters. The party in the station's rec room wound down and shortly only one man was left, finishing his beer, checking ashtrays and soon he turned off the record player and staggered to bed.

At 0700 hours there was a console shift change and then all quiet as a mouse until the cook's helper started coffee at ten. Some hardy souls arrived for bacon and eggs at eleven after which the kitchen staff began preparations for a turkey dinner to be followed by a new movie, *It's a Wonderful Life*, that Manny had set aside to fill in the day-long festivities.

At 1400 hours there were a lot of footsteps in the halls, which prompted a few guys to leave their sacks. Why would anyone run anywhere? Young Simon was in the rec room with a wild story about all the people in the duplex being sick.

'Puking, half blind, very bad.'

He had tried for a long time but he couldn't wake Simon or Annie or Big Tooth and would Qallunaag, the white man, come now, come now, please.

Before Manny could ask any questions, young Simon was doubled up in a lot of pain and then cancelled the idea of a movie in the rec room that night by puking all over the floor. Morry Kaplan, the first-aid man, Manny and the lead radician, Paul Doucette, gathered up blankets and a gallon of grapefruit juice that Morry swore would cure any hangover, and they roared off to the Inuit housing.

The entry door was wide open and light from inside spilled out across the white snow. Old Simon, dressed in red long johns, appeared to be sleeping for he was curled up on a mound of snow beside the front door. Morry and Paul tried to move him inside but the body was as hard and cold as the mound it rested on. Going through the door, a rank, raw, seal skin smell stopped them momentarily, and then a different odor – alcohol, even stronger than the smell of fish, raw skins and vomit.

A fast check of the two rooms produced a body count of five adults needing or beyond medical aid and three small almond-eyed kids who were moved out of there speedily. The ugly job of sorting bodies and giving aid kept the men busy. Two of the people, Mary and Eddy, were loaded on to the truck almost before it stopped on its return trip after delivering the kids to the site.

Due to the open door, the normally comfortable living room had become a walk-in freezer and in a very short time, the grotesque bodies were too stiff to rearrange and it was decided to leave things as they were. The heat was turned down and the lights and the record player, still belting out Hank Snow, were turned off and the door closed to await the Mounties, who, hopefully, would arrive the next day.

On the second day of the new year, the sun arrived at 7:22 A.M. and the Royal Canadian Mounted plane arrived at 9:45 A.M. The investigation began immediately, and by 1100 hours they were in possession of all the relative facts. Prior to the evening of December 31, the indigenous population at the Federal Electric site, known as Cam Two, had neither been instructed about, nor introduced to, the fluid called de-icer and they had not been cautioned as to the toxic nature of the fluid de-icer. They had, in fact, misinterpreted jesting remarks recently made by white co-workers, that the fluid was a beneficial agent. It was thought by the Eskimos that white members of a recent work party had made common use of the toxic fluid as a party beverage.

What it boiled down to was that when Simon and Peter ran out of store-bought booze on New Year's morning, they had made a trip and come back with some of Qallunaags' blue whisky. Within the hour, the tea and de-icer cocktail had laid out three of their number. The kids tried a cup but it was more like white gas than soda pop so they drank less than a mouthful. Mary and Eddy had taken theirs straight, vomited almost immediately and did themselves the favor of passing out.

With the completion of the informal inquest, the Mounties went home to Cambridge Bay. Manny assigned Morry and Paul to the temporary positions of site assistant casket builders and Andre Qapelle, the Cam Two 'J' mechanic, would oversee the construction of the five plywood coffins.

'Use plenty of nails. We don't want them coming apart in transit.'

The semi-skilled woodworkers measured, cut and assembled the coffin-shaped shipping crates in the hangar where a new shipment of plywood was conveniently stacked. The five shrunken Inuit bodies were wrapped in blankets and comfortably arranged, and two days later, on January 5, the *Arctic Rose* taxied up to the Cam Two hangar doors.

A quiet subdued group of men assisted with the loading and after the rough coffins had been carried aboard and cargo nets had been installed, securing the load, the five walking Inuit boarded. The co-pilot and Manny guided Eddy up the steps for he was blind. The three children, no smiles, no shy grins, clustered close to the hobbling Aunt Mary.

The white men watched the empty sky, the drooping windsock and the empty landscape. When the plane had gone, taking the crippled, the dead and the innocent to Winnipeg for further investigation, they piled into Manny's truck and returned to the routine of Cam Two.

In February, head office instructed Manny to forward those surplus drums of de-icer listed on the current inventory. A recent audit had revealed that Cam Two had seven forty-five-gallon drums in stock. That was two hundred and twenty-five gallons in excess of station requirements.

Manny replied that the audit was correct but a thorough check of the POL farm had been conducted and it had been ascertained that the current de-icer inventory was nil.

I can offer no reasonable explanation for this discrepancy.
M. Bitman
Station Chief

Chapter Eight

Doc transferred to Foxe Main two months prior to the commissioning of the Foxe-Thule Troppo-Scatter system. Doc had joined a new team, the Foxe-Thule Troppo system technicians. He was assigned quarters in the lower camp D train. A camp bed in an empty room, with a worn linoleum floor covering, a hanging, naked light bulb and half a mile to the dining room. This was the wrong side of the tracks. Salt mine treatment. Quartering techs in these barracks; hey now, get real.

The team leader was Lee Turska who had been born in Montana thirty-five years earlier. He was ex-USN (United States Navy) and had spent two years as a communications officer running a surveillance operation from a retrofitted destroyer in the Yellow Sea. On occasion, he referred to this duty as his Korean pooper-snooper tour.

He insisted that the Canadians who maintained this six-hundred-mile microwave hop should be top drawer and he would suffer none of the bullshit-baffles-brain adherents on his team. Lee perused the performance review files of radicians, radio technicians, super technicians and even the go-for-coffee Carrier technicians and the result of this screening was that Troppo team members were the cream of the Federal Electric troubleshooters. One man was passed over when Lee found a commendation in the man's dossier stating that here was, *A pearl in these sands of ignorance*. Lee added a footnote: *This beauty should not be wasted on mortal endeavors*.

The super team was selected from all sectors of the line transferred from east and west or in the instance of reluctant volunteerism, shanghaied. One warm body, returning from R and R at the time of his capture by the 'Turska press gang', arrived at Foxe without shirts, shorts or socks and worse, dead broke. But enough of the fun and games.

The carpenters, electricians, plumbers and painters rebuilt the team's living quarters and D train could now be used as a representative model for the spring issue of *Good Housekeeping* magazine. Orientation and familiarization began. Lee 'The Boss' Turska demanded that they knew, to the milliamp, what was normal at hundreds of test points. The men spent weeks with the schematics and only when 'The Boss' was satisfied that comprehension was total did they move to hands-on familiarization. 'The Boss' hated paperwork and was not about to spend a lot of time completing a fault report because some guy had tripped an on-air radio. The training was intense, which resulted in a coherent team of professionals.

Tropospheric Scatter is a method of transmitting microwaves over long distances. A microwave path in southern climes is a nominal twenty-five miles but if these microwaves are bounced off the troposphere, distances of six hundred miles can be realized.

Scatter system microwaves are rather like car headlights in thick fog. The light penetrates but diffuses, but small amounts can still be utilized. Scatter systems are high power, up to one million watts and employ very large antenna structures for more efficient recovery of the highly diffused radio waves. The billboard antennas at the Foxe-Thule site are one hundred and fifty feet high and two hundred feet long and the microwave radiation in the front of these towering concave faces will sterilize a man a mile away on the tundra.

The Thule site, as it came to be called, was built two miles from the main site, a satellite village. The ponderous steel-sided building, a bulge on the tundra, was dwarfed in the shadows of the antennas.

The training period was a pleasant change from previous DEW-line duty: new equipment, an eight to five shift and a boss who knew the score. The training was complete, Lee was satisfied and the team was ready. No one was about to reduce a $10,000 klystron transmitting tube to a two-ton puddle of molten glass and copper.

The shift schedules were posted and the boys settled into routine operations. A blue crew cab truck was assigned to the project and each man received two years' supply of timesheets and a safe driving handbook. All systems were normal. The stream of visiting MIT (Massachusetts Institute of Technology) and Lenkurt and USAF trickled down to the occasional once-a-week stop and coffee break visit by the garbage truck driver named Jack. Jack would arrive at the side door and, after coffee and a cigarette, haul the week's accumulation of garbage somewhere else.

In early times, during construction, the site had been littered with scrap material, packing cases, crates and wrapping paper. All manner of debris had littered the immediate area. The team had no time to manicure the front lawn and greens-keeping of the tundra was left for later. This was the land of no trees and before winter ice arrived, natives of the neighboring village salvaged the cases, crates and even the splinters. In exchange for this great wealth they groomed the entire area.

During the last days of construction, a pack of loose dogs frequented the area but after the clean-up they were infrequently seen. Doc had been on hand the day of the clean-up and had set two of the stout boxes aside. He was not an accumulator but during the long night, who knows, he might need some book shelves or maybe materials for trade.

In November, Doc started feeding a silver-furred pregnant bitch. This was a no-no, a definite do not do and with good reason, for several men had been badly bitten by these bellicose animals. There had been several incidents of men feeding them scraps and when the man went south the dogs became a confused, hungry nuisance. Nevertheless, Doc fell for another female sob story.

The bitch began putting on weight and it became apparent that she was pregnant. Her manner with Doc was that of guarded acceptance and he construed this as real friendly. With the other technicians, there were snarls, growls and bared teeth, all of which Doc explained as good taste. Doc placed one of the salvaged crates at the shipping door where it was sheltered from the prevailing west wind and away from public eyes. During the next month the bitch defined a ten-foot area that was off limits to everyone but Doc. The boundary was accorded great respect after Ron Currie swore the bitch was going for his throat the day he attempted a short cut to the garbage bins.

The work routine kept the crew busy and Doc became very upbeat when the countdown to his R and R passed thirty days. Twenty-nine days to be exact.

'Jeez, this has to be the fastest tour yet.'

That same day, the bitch gave birth to five pups. It was eight days before Doc saw them, a moving, wobbling, droop-eared, fur throng of tails and feet. They stayed close to the dinner table. The bitch brooked no wandering explorations by her brood nor transgressions by would-be puppy-petting technicians. Doc dropped the day's offering in front of her and the watching head showed some teeth and growled. Doc told the boys that she was back to her old self but he was wise enough not to test the friendship.

With three weeks to go, Doc's R and R plans began firming up and this time he would make it back to see the folks. Mum and Dad had a forty-acre tree farm west of Calgary and a visit was long overdue. He and Michael Clow had made some tentative Mexican slurp and burp tour plans but they were flexible. They would spend some time in Calgary then on to Mexico. There was an idea about the pups, some details to sort through. Details, details.

Four new men arrived and began their Thule Troppo orientation. They brought some new jokes and different small talk, which was a nice change. None of the new men pushed introductions on the bitch after the first hostile reception.

Doc heard from the folks and Mum saw no problem if Stanley – Doc's Christian name – were to bring home an authentic Arctic husky.

Not a vicious one, dear, and it should be male for they're so much easier to manage. Dad can build a kennel of some sort and it will be comforting to have a watchdog about the place.

Doc checked with the Polar Aire dispatcher and made arrangements to take a pup on board when he headed south on the twenty-fourth, two weeks hence. He asked some of the guys on the Troppo team about hauling steak bones, scraps, diet supplements, but the consensus was expressed by Ron Currie.

'Will the bitch know the difference between a steak bone and the arm offering it?'

Smiling Jack still showed up for coffee and occasionally he would haul away some garbage. Jack and Doc spent some time in discussion about the bitch and her progeny.

'To whom does the bitch belong?'

'Anybody, everybody, who cares?'

'How come they don't freeze up solid in winter?'

'Get serious.'

'So tell me, Happy. What happens to stray dogs?'

Jack shrugged his shoulders at that one. His conversation leaned more to things commercial.

'You want a real good fox skin? I got one, real cheap, ten bucks or two bucks and four beer.'

When Doc pressed Jack about the dogs, Jack said, 'I got skidoo. I don't catch fish all summer to feed dog all winter.'

Doc found time to make a small hand carry case from scrounged material. The deluxe pet cage required two days to build. It had two coats of paint and the interior was thickly padded – a custom-built pup house with air holes and a hinged lid.

Three days before the DC-4 was due to take Doc south the dogs disappeared. Doc had arranged to work the afternoon shift on his last week and when he arrived at the Troppo building at 1430 hours, the nursery crate was empty. It was routine for him to feed the bitch as he came to work and she would growl her pleasure but this time there was an empty crate, a chewed-on bone beside the tipped-over water dish and silence. Doc got down on his knees and peered into the shadows of the crate. Nothing there except a doggy odor.

He walked to the front of the steel building and then completed the circle looking for tracks or dogs or something. No dogs, nothing, except the damned wind still blowing cold off the ice-cap.

The next day, Doc wrangled the Troppo team truck and cruised the tundra in a ten-mile circle around the site. It was slow going in low gear and at 1400 hours, with an almost empty gas tank, he gave up. It didn't make sense. Where the hell could she have got to with those pups? Not far in the forty-knot wind that had been blowing for the last week.

Those damned village dogs must have got her, he thought. The Eskimos never feed those animals and a pack of them showed up at the crate and had her and the pups for lunch.

The next day was spent packing and cleaning up the room. At the end of the shift, Doc sprang for a forty-ounce bottle of rye and at about 2:00 A.M., a bottle of Hennessy Three Star came out of hiding. They shook Doc awake at 0800 hours.

'The Polar Aire flight is an hour out and you'd better get some shorts on.'

He was not the usual neat, debonair, bouncy Doc. His enemies would have called him hung-over and he admitted to feeling a bit shaky. Eddy, the dispatcher slipped him a beer when he arrived at the hangar and with a measure of discreetness he departed for the men's toilet. He had barely finished the inhalation when Smiling Jack looked in.

'Hi, Doc. You go south, sure?'

'Ya, going on some holiday.'

'My wife, Jeannie, she make real nice mukluks. You buy?'

'I don't think so, Jack. There's no extra money right now.'

'Ten bucks, Doc. They real good. Here, you look.'

Jack pulled the soft-soled, hand-decorated, fur-trimmed native boots out of a pocket and Doc took them for a closer examination. They were new, not fully tanned and the smell of the almost green leather caused an instant reawakening of Doc's stomach disorders.

'Ah, look, Jack, they're nice, real nice, but not today. When I get back. Okay?'

'Doc, they your size. Jeannie made them for you. She sewed all night and she say you buy. Okay?'

'Well, okay, okay. Here.'

Doc gave Jack ten dollars and jammed the brown and purple footwear into his carry-on flight bag, down to the bottom beside the emergency half pint.

'Well, I'll see you, Jack. Thank Jeannie, and I'll see you in three weeks.'

Doc boarded and cinched up the seatbelt. An hour later he woke with a pounding head and furry tongue. He groped in the bottom of the flight bag and dug out the half pint of 'medicine'. It helped but another smell reminded him of his recent purchase. He pulled the brown and purple mukluks out and took time to examine them with a more critical eye. The soft fur trim was nice, very nice. An unusual silver color, not wolverine or deer. Maybe wolf. No, the fur is something else. Almost like dog but where the hell would he get dog fur? Jack makes a point about dogs being too much trouble. He has a skidoo and no dogs. Oh shit! My pups, damn his eyes! He's charged me ten bucks for my pups!

Chapter Nine

During the nine months of winter, time on the line slowed to a crawl. The outside air was too fresh and the stuff in the dorms and work areas became a stale, stagnate substance that was only partly revitalized by the door openings of men on work-related assignments.

Those who worked the Foxe-Thule Troppo system ventured the two miles between their work center and the main site with some enjoyment in escaping, even briefly, the odorous traces of diesel fumes, chemical toilets and sour socks. The fumes of Doc's cheap cigars permeated recreation and dining room but the stink could be dissipated in the Troppo truck by the judicious opening of a small side window during the ten-minute ride to and from the site. The Troppo building air was a comfortable, air-conditioned, seventy-two degrees Fahrenheit. Large fans circulated vast amounts of outside air through the building as a primary coolant and this air was definitely fresh.

It had been thought that the large amounts of raw radio power generated by the megawatt klystrons would cause problems during repairs to the sensitive test equipment, and that a shielded structure would isolate the test bench area from the klystron-generated noise and spurious magnetic fields. Some consultation with contractors, site engineers and architectural draughtsmen resulted in a distinctive modification to the Troppo building.

The resulting structure was immediately identified as the 'cage'. A twenty by twenty foot, wire mesh-enclosed structure, built for the purpose of test and calibration of electronic test equipment. Three-foot-wide workbenches lined the inside walls, a profusion of electrical outlets added a surrealistic border and a multitudinous array of overhead lights made this a unique structure.

The benches were seldom used and more and more the empty enclosure was utilized by the Troppo team as a personal hobby shop. There was little else to do. Write home, a game of bumper pool in the rec room and every eight hours another meal. One escapade that Doc and Doug Little engineered was the reply to a 'Sir Gent' advertisement: 'Attention lonely men. Young attractive girls of Asian extraction will enter into the exchange of correspondence with mature males.'

A Manila post office box number was the return address. Bruce Hendley, a recent addition to the Troppo team, was selected as the recipient by a unanimous vote of two.

'I tell you, Doc, he's lonely.'

'Well, Doug, do you have proof? No specific details, but something besides shaving twice a day.'

'Sure. After he shaves, with a real razor I might add, he uses aftershave lotion.'

'It's not that I doubt you, Doug, but you have been in a long time. He may be trying to get a steady job.'

'Doc, he needs help. He flosses between meals.'

A self-addressed envelope with a recent picture of Bruce brought a gratifying response – two hundred and forty-seven letters addressed to B. Hendley. The subject matter of the contents varied between citizenship, marriage, and solicitations for Canadian funds, that would be applied to future postage. Three letters were very frank about the exotic delights that young ladies, of Catholic upbringing no less, could offer. Bruce blushed, stammered, and proceeded to answer every one.

For those who were big on building models, the hot items were motor driven cars: Corvettes, Ferraris and drag strip roadsters had all been reduced to white plastic replicas. Three hours to glue the pieces together and another sixty hours would be spent hand-painting racing stripes and adding miniature Good-Year, Motorcraft and Penzoil decals. For a few dollars more, the aficionado could have a full figure of eight track with a rheostat and hand controls, and the next step in the logical progression, parallel tracks with starting gates, pit stops and finish line. A complete miniaturized speedway.

The track started small but grew. The miniature machines, powered by small nine-volt DC (direct current) motors lacked only the blue-black exhaust smoke and the roar of a super-charged Oppenheimer engine for authenticity. The momentary hush at the start, the roar of the crowd, and even a slight whiff of oil in the air, added to the Saturday night raceway feeling at the Foxe Main Five Hundred.

The 'cage' had changed since its austere beginnings. The wide worktop-high benches now supported dual oval tracks that were equipped with an electronic start barrier and an ultraviolet light finish line. The chicken-wire ceiling had been cloth draped to keep dust off the tracks, and rows of neon lights eliminated shadows. Pit crew areas, a daily events board, Bardohl and Castor oil posters all contributed to the speedway atmosphere.

The half-mile post was actually thirty feet from the starting line and the three-quarter mile, mile and mile-and-a-quarter posts were similarly scaled out around the track's perimeter. The two tracks utilized a common starting switch and the races were supervised by an impartial observer, a very rare bird indeed. A light beam had been installed for timing, rear end weighting raised the track record, and the competition became ever more intense. Talk of two-motor systems, bevel gears and speed controllers dominated dinner conversation. Starting with equivalent building materials and almost identical building expertise the racing time of the entrants slowly approached a dead-heat situation.

The most intense competition developed between the Troppo team cars and main site radicians' entries. More specifically, between Doc's *Mexican Sunrise* and a beautifully miniaturized Corvette raced by Gordon 'Fat Boy' Shockton, the lead radician.

Fat Boy was not a friendly dude. He was big, overweight to the point of 'belly over belt' and his personality was always contemptuous. He was a competent technician but there was an arrogance. He disdained to run his car in any of the preliminary heats choosing, instead, to make a grandiose entrance at 2200 hours. His assertion for inclusion in final heats caused loud words and awkward situations, but by bluster and cajolery he would eventually have his way.

A third car, Doug Little's *Purple Patute*, a superbly crafted miniaturization of a California street rod, was another of the top seed. Invariably, the three would race to determine the night's championship. Such was the situation until Doc spent an afternoon of his time off puttering about in the 'cage'.

'Just swamping out some crud,' was his explanation.

On Friday evening, Doc inveigled Doug to bet fifty dollars. Doug would have been the first to admit that beating *Mexican Sunrise* was no sure thing but Doc's contention was that he would do it by five seconds! No way. Doug was aware of Doc's recent scratching around for money. Something about the Eskimo kids and the village priest. Too bad. Doug had plans for some Manila ladies and an extra fifty would be very nice spending during the forthcoming time of refreshment and reconstruction.

'Cars, take your positions, drivers start your engines and the race is on and at the half-mile post we have...'

A tabloid description of the race would have been, 'A multicolored blur swept to a clean ten-second victory over a valiant but outclassed California, *Purple Patute.*'

Doug yelled foul, but after extensive checking the race committee could find no reason to disallow the victory. Doug asked for time to pay the bet for he was taking vacation in two weeks and would honor this indebtedness when he returned.

'I'd like to oblige you, Doug,' said Doc. 'We've been friends for quite awhile, working partners, you name it, but what would I tell the next guy? But, there is something, a small matter that we could look at.'

Doc, Doug and invited guests retired to the Troppo team bar where Doc lavishly bought drinks all around. When the time was appropriate he explained the winning technique. The men in attendance were skeptical but one and all made their way two miles back across the tundra to test their racers using Doc's innovation. It was a fact. There was a twenty-five percent improvement in all models except for the 'Frisco Public Transportation vehicle' which caught fire, but Doc, with great presence, extinguished the conflagration before the track suffered any permanent damage.

The next step was obvious. The radicians had been making big noises about the superior quality and the peerless performance of the cheeseboxes they had stuffed together. It was time to find out how sincere they were about those extravagant claims. The hook was set during the following week. Breakfast, lunch and dinner conversations delved into the speed of Doc's machine. It was rumored that (a) he had sandpapered the drive wheels, (b) he had received special racing wheels from Mattel, the manufacturer of all the kits that had been built, or (c), that by balancing with weights, front and rear, he had achieved a breakthrough and was going to patent the idea. The last rumor was discarded by those in the know because weighting was a common practice. It was conceded that the Troppo guys were bullshitting. This was a con, but no one could figure out how.

The betting was getting heavy and Gordon, 'Fat Boy' Shockton was leading the parade. Doug Little showed up at the radicians' after-hours watering hole on Tuesday night. He had finished his last shift and was flying south in the morning but it was obvious that the holiday had begun several hours earlier. The reception was cool when he arrived at the radicians' oasis but being men of similar hungers, he was allowed entrance.

'Fat Boy' Shockton's bets were approaching two hundred bucks, and although he would never admit it, he was worried. But what goes around comes around, and here was a guy who had just been sucked in by Doc, and he just might spill something useful.

'How's the drink, Doug?' Shockton asked. 'I've got some over-proof rum here that'll knock you on your well known. I might as well tell you, I think you know how we can win your fifty bucks back. Right? And you think I'm the guy who can do it.'

'Rum sounds fine, Gord, mighty fine and let's get the bullshit out of the way. Okay? I don't begrudge Doc that fifty. He always had a better machine.'

'Sure, but what made him think it was five seconds faster? I don't want to run Doc down, hell, I've known him for years but I don't see how he can make those Dinky toys run that fast without some gimmick. I know him and he's being cute. So what do you say, Doug? Let's win back your fifty? You and me.'

'Gordon, old buddy, say pour a little more of that rum syrup in here. Gordon, I'm going to let you in on a little secret. You ain't got a hope in hell of beating Doc with that second string race machine of yours.' Doug nodded wisely and repeated, 'Not a hope in hell.'

'Screw you, Doug, I've beaten everything on the site at one time or another. You haven't heard about it but last month I got myself a new high-traction rear wheel kit, a new idea from Mattel and now, well, I have the fastest machine.'

'Gord, old buddy, I'm impressed, but face it, Doc is a little smarter than the average bear. What you should do is come to Manila with me.' Doug sipped more rum and continued, 'I got me some of the damnedest phone numbers and I've got the names of half the dames in some convent or other and let me tell you… they sound wild.'

'What's he got, Doug?' Gordon persisted. 'Here, that glass needs a little juice. Tell me, partner, what's so special about Doc's machine?'

Doug took another taste of the rum and there he sat with an owlish solemnity. Finally he said, 'Partners right? Okay, it's not the car, it's the track.'

'The track, the track, what the hell do you mean? The track.'

'Doc rigged the track,' Doug said. 'He raised the voltage. We got parallel tracks down there and most guys use the first track. You've done it. Set your model down on the closest track and the second track sits, waiting for the competition. First guy picks the track. Well, what Doc has done is add a second power supply, for the second track. When they turn on the track power, they turn on two power supplies.'

'Well, I'll be… That sneaky fox.'

'So now you know and we're partners, right? You bet fifty bucks for me and this is just between you and me. I'll be back and I'll be working with these guys. So easy does it.'

'Don't worry,' Gordon reassured him. 'This is you and me. We'll clean up. Would you believe it? Some of the radicians have been betting against me! It's going to be a pleasure to teach those bastards a lesson.'

'So what about my fifty bucks? I'll be on R and R. I'm going south tomorrow.'

'I'll get it down, don't worry. You'll have it when you get back. Just you, me and Corvette makes three. Hot damn.'

Saturday night arrangements for transportation to the Thule Troppo building were negotiated all through dinner. By 1900 hours everyone from Vern, the head cook, to Morris, the 'J' mechanic, had made some deal for taxi service. By 2100 hours, the long dormitory halls were empty and the only sign of life was the pulsing throb of the diesel generators. At the Troppo building parking lot every vehicle assigned to the Foxe Main site had been abandoned in the vehicle turnaround area. Beyond the cone of light that marked the double door main entrance, dog teams could be seen tethered on the snow-blown tundra.

Inside, the overhead lights were dimmed and in the open central area a crowd of men milled around the brightly lit 'cage'. Talk noise rose and fell and the occasional clink of glass against glass mixed with snatches of 'You asshole, get off my…' and 'It'll be good for it on payday'. The wire-enclosed area of the 'cage' was spacious, free of the crowd of shoulder-to-shoulder men. Only contestants were allowed entry.

An argument between Doc and 'Fat Boy' was resolved when Doc conceded that visitors had the pick of the starting gates. Pressure by the entire assembly had forced Doc to relinquish this much of the normal procedures and, at last, both cars were in position. Behind them, the starter slapped two boards together to produce a satisfying pistol-like sound and the cars tore out of their start positions together. The finish was pandemonium personified.

'Two out of three. You agreed, you suggested it. Two out of three!' Doc was yelling, nose to 'Fat Boy's nose. 'Two out of three!'

With a condescending wave of his hand and an 'Okay, okay', 'Fat Boy' positioned the candy-red model in the starting gate of the winning track. Doc gave him a hard look and mumbled something, setting *Mexican Sunrise* into position. He spent long minutes checking and rechecking the track for dust and more time was used inspecting the electrical wiper that connected his model to the power rail. At last he turned to Shockton.

'You want to double that bet, Gordon? Double or nothing?'

'Christ, Doc. That would make it five hundred.'

'So, are you a windbag or what? Go for broke I say.'

'Screw you, Doc. Five hundred it is, and payable tonight.'

Slowly a wave of silence engulfed the crowd. Some of the men in the back rows were standing on chairs.

'Down in front. Down in front,' and then the pistol-shot bang of the boards being slammed together.

Around and around, a slight slackening of pace at the corners and the last lap and the finish line and then, bedlam… *Mexican Sunrise* had won by two lengths, and Gordon 'Fat Boy' Shockton was dumbfounded for it was the same track, the same car. He turned to his sidekick, Jason Calder.

'What the hell is going on? Did you see anything? What the hell did that bastard do?'

Doc allowed time for Doug's stutter to moderate, and then with an almost gentle smile, said, 'Two out of three, Mr. Shockton.'

Doc's glasses glittered in the overhead neon; the worried look was gone and here was Doctor Rafferty, the maestro.

'Well, sir, shall we race? Pick a track. Show us your stuff. Perhaps you were teasing us with the last run, hmm?' Turning to the crowd, he continued, 'It's like I keep telling you, boys. Craftsmanship will always triumph, superior craftsmanship. That and superior intelligence.'

'Okay, okay, lard butt, knock off the crap. You got lucky with that garbage can this time.'

Gordon again placed his deluxe model in the illicit starting position. He checked electrical connections and lightly touched up the rear wheels with an emery cloth and now he was ready to race. Doc in turn performed the same ministrations to his model, but there was a devilish smile not hidden by cigar smoke. The bang of the boards and the cars were away.

At the Troppo team's dorm the station complement wandered in and out of the open doorways. The Troppo gang had sprung for the booze and there was laughter and loud yells. Doc had commandeered the end room, the one with the phone. He was talking long-distance to Winnipeg.

'Just like we figured, Doug. He bet the farm. Thought he was on the hot track. He's so goddamned arrogant. He wouldn't take the time to figure out we could switch the higher voltage to either track, not him.' He stopped talking to listen and then said, 'You could say he was upset, you could say that. Daimler, right, Father Daimler was there and the winnings went to the Eskimo kids' Christmas party. Well, sure, it's not for awhile but anyway he handed out receipts for the donations so everybody gets a tax write-off. I'll hold yours till you get back. You'll be back, old buddy, that is if those Filipino señoritas don't kill you.'

Chapter Ten

At ten past seven on Monday morning, Vince drained the bottom of his coffee cup, meticulously patted his silver moustache dry, brushed invisible crumbs from his chin and departed the Foxe Main upper camp dining room. This would be a fine day for he, Vincent J. O'Neil, would, if necessary, make it so.

Vince was the DEW-line Foxe sector POL (petroleum oil lubricants) specialist and was responsible for all petroleum products used in the Foxe sector; petroleum products including Av gas, truck gas, paint remover, de-icer, gear oil, diesel fuel, etcetera. The largest item on his analogous inventory was item ANAF (Army, Navy, Air Force) 6100-75682/002, commonly called diesel fuel. Each fall, two twenty-five-thousand-gallon beach tanks were filled with diesel fuel from a Montreal dispatched oil tanker and there would be no further fuel delivered for twelve months.

In the two years that Vince had been the POL specialist there had been increasing demands for diesel and because of this greater demand, Vince had requisitioned and installed fuel cell bladders on the beach. The bladder bags, like rubberized giant Chicklets, proved to be a perfect solution for temporary storage with their large, five-thousand-gallon capacity and low profile to minimize snowdrift build-up.

When the Montreal tanker arrived and was safely anchored half a mile offshore, Vince and his crew would fill the large main tanks on the beach. Next the in-use tanks at the site were pumped full and then several smaller tanks at the motor pool garage were topped off and then there were the bladder bags on the beach. All in all, about a hundred thousand gallons. Vince used the fuel from the bladder bags first and as they emptied, transferred to pumping the main reserves. This left a small amount of diesel in the pipes of the now idle temporary system. Demands on Vince's time had prevented pumping the system for the residual fuel. He estimated eight hundred, maybe a thousand gallons remained in the half a mile of interconnecting two-inch-diameter pipe. The first thing would be to open the secondary bypass valves which were electrical. Thank God. Then activate the pumps, followed by a thorough check of the lines. Please God, don't let there be any water in those lines…

A mile away at the Foxe Main lower camp kitchen, breakfast was over and the grunts were climbing across benches into the aisles. A normal morning exodus. No one had moved until the morning cook had yelled, 'Get your asses outa here,' and now they were pushing and shoving and pulling on parkas and gloves at the open annex doors.

The cold air pouring in made clouds around the men and earned another yell from the cook, and finally the only man left was MacGonigle, a large ponderous hulk with a red nose stuck on the crags of a purple-splotched face. He sat quietly, preparing the ten-inch cigar that he would absorb that day. When the cigar was fully blackened by applications of spit, it was clamped in the corner of Mac's mouth. During the next eight hours, it would shrink and at 2100 hours all that would remain would be a half-inch black button stuck in the same corner of his mouth.

In the annex, Mac stomped, grungy, wool sock-clad feet into shapeless ten-year-old snow boots, donned a non-regulation fleece-lined parka, left undone because of a broken zipper. He acknowledged a nip in the thirty-below air by covering his bald head with a red toque and pulling the rolled rim level with his bushy eyebrows. With his personal adjustments completed, he rolled out of the dining room to the truck idling ten feet away. Mac claimed the truck had been assigned to him by no less than an American Air Force inspector general.

With casual skill he drove through windblown tendrils of drifted snow to the airport hangar. During the day, Mac would plow the overnight accumulation of two- and three-foot-high snowdrifts, banked across this road, the upper camp road and the airport runway. It would be a short eight-hour day and the toughest part would be starting the six-hundred-horsepower diesel engine of the plow-equipped road grader.

Mac referred to this mechanized monster as the 'Blue Smoke, Belching Bugger', which he had wisely parked in the heated hangar. In times of severe winds and extreme drifting, Mac would roll the red toque rim down over his ears and walk the half-mile to the hangar. On this day the air was calm and the sun, a red ball, rose above the eastern sea ice into a clear sky and the overnight drifts were at a minimum. It was shaping up to be a damned fine day, damned fine.

Above the Sixtieth Parallel, the prevailing winds are north to south and knowing the north wind will blow the runway clear is a determining factor when constructing airport runways, terrain permitting. The terrain at Foxe Main had not permitted and two large lakes and the Arctic Ocean had dictated an east–west strip that packed with snow from the first winds of winter.

Day after winter day, Mac moved snow from the runway's north side to the south side where the wind picked it up again to carry it, some said, as far as Portage and Main in Winnipeg – an exaggeration. It rarely went past Churchill. This day was no different. There were snowdrifts across the runway and Mac was still on the first pass when Vince drove up beside the plow.

'I'm going to need some help, Mac. I want to clean out the oil dregs left in the bladder bags and then flush the lines. Will you drive your plow down there, and open up the temporary valves?'

'Sure. I can do that. Make a change in scenery.'

Vince thanked Mac and added, 'Those lines will have air in them. I keep them pressurized to keep water out.'

'No sweat, Vince. You get ready to start the pumps. I have my mobile and I'll call you when I get to the beach. Okay?'

'Sounds good. Remember, you have to come back up the road to open a valve at the main line junction.'

'Right. I'll be there in about an hour.'

The bladder tank farm's two-inch oil line was temporary. It had been constructed on pedestals, three feet above the tundra, and red-flagged every twenty yards. Vince planned to spend a lot of time installing a permanent system before the next sea-lift, when the weather was more amiable.

Early in the game Mac realized that a lot of the red flags had blown away. Missing markers were no problem for Mac. He knew the temporary line as well as Vince, at least he knew where the line had been. During the sea-lift a greenhorn driver had added a dog-leg to the beach road and what had been a straight line from the bladder bags to the main control valve was no more. The shortest distance application had been abandoned by a fully loaded supply truck that had broken through the beach road tundra and the subsequent excavation of the truck had caused a small detour. Nothing much, two yards to the left, two yards to the right and back to the original track. Summer help had repaired the pipeline. They had laid the new pipe beside the now dog-legged road. Red flags! What the hell for? Vince intended to correct the deviation when the weather was more amiable. The line moved oil so why sweat it?

Mac and his yellow machine moved in stately grace along the seldom-used track, cleaving drifts of three and four feet in height. The engine's melodic roar was a symphony of sound to Mac's tin ear. Mac's eyes occasionally wandered from the line of red markers to the distant horizon, where blue snow crystals sparkled like diamonds beneath a benevolent sun. What a damned fine day.

Mac was inspecting the 'damned fine day' when the snowplow's steel blade cut the two-inch temporary pipe, full of oil, and the crystal-bright day now became an oil-splashed mess. A lot of mess. Mac hollered into the mobile radio and after a lot of yelling back and forth, Vince turned off the pumps and the pulsing black stream slowed to a gurgle.

From the ragged end of the twisted pipe the last few drops plopped in the black, slowly widening circle. Oil ran down the sides of the machine and a black trail followed the splattered equipment as it backed away from the ten-foot-wide blot in the white snow. Slowly the grader lurched away back down the track.

That morning, Sammy Maniapic had stayed on the sleeping platform and enjoyed the warmth of the Hudson Bay blankets. His wife Mary had lit the oil stove and Sammy had pampered himself until the government-built, one-room house had begun to warm. There was very little fuel. Enough to cook with and if Mary was thrifty there were occasions when they could squander a small amount for warming the house itself.

For the past two days there had been no snow and this was good. The sea ice was now windswept and clear and he could drive his put-put machine many miles in hunt for seal. With the ice now snow free, he would find the seals' breathing holes and this could mean a week's supply of seal meat and heating oil. Each year there were fewer seals in the shallow offshore waters. During the past summer, only three seals had been taken by this village of thirty-six people. Blue eyes at the Hudson Bay store would trade oil for fox, but this winter, even foxes were scarce.

'Aye, the wind has gone and this is good. Today will be good, aye, very good.'

Sammy, on his way to the hoped-for sleeping seals, witnessed Mac sever the pipeline. Call him 'Sammy on the spot'. Astonished, he sat with open mouth, seals forgotten. He was quick to recover. He made a racing U-turn away from the calamity and, while oil still dripped from the pipe, Sammy was heading back to the 'people' and before another pot of tea was brewed a circus had been organized and was headed over the tundra: dog sledges, skidoos, kids' sledging sleds and toboggans, all with forty-five-gallon drums or washtubs, dishpans, bedpans or empty wine jars. The fuel oil salvage had begun.

Radar site consoles were manned on a twenty-four-hour basis and the operator's prime duty was the constant observation of an oscilloscope. Hopefully, the oscilloscope's green and white display would change and the wide-awake operator would note the passage of machines flying through that segment of sky being 'swept' by the electronic system attached to the visual display. A secondary function performed by the radician on duty was to monitor the mobile radio in the event that some more mundane vehicle might need assistance; to be pulled out of a snow bank would be such a case.

On the morning of the great pipeline blow out, Michael Clow, recently transferred from Cam Two, had caught the morning console and had overheard much of the mobile radio traffic; strange conversations concerning pipelines and pumps. When his shift ended he located a truck that would not be missed and shortly he was driving the newly plowed road to the beach. The end of the road was organized bedlam. All the people of the village had come: grandmothers, grandfathers, dads, uncles, small children, large children. They were dressed in blue parkas and green parkas and red parkas and multi-combinations of color, parkas.

Women in flower-patterned garb were shoveling snow and men with fur-trimmed parkas were shoveling snow. The children were playing a new game of filling barrels and three dog teams, still hitched to long Inuit freight sleds, added to the confusion. Two black and yellow skidoos, with toboggans tied to the back bumpers, were parked with the dogs. The Inuit were shoveling oil-soaked snow into the barrels, pots and pans, and as the vessels were filled they were driven away in the direction of the village. The work party ignored the truck's arrival and only Sammy acknowledged Michael's presence by asking for a cigarette. The two stood quietly, watching. The Inuit had an ear-to ear grin.

Shortly Michael asked, 'What do you do with it? The snow.'

'Oh, very good snow. When snow dries up, there will be oil, lots of oil. Okay?'

Michael was still puzzled but said, 'Sure, guess so.'

'Damned right, damned right. Lots of oil for heat. Maybe enough oil for all year. Today is very good. I must help now but you come anytime. Anytime and we tea up. Okay.'

'Thanks. I'll do that.'

By 2100 hours Mac and Vince had finished a preliminary debriefing of the situation. The meeting had taken place in Mac's room, which was located in the B train of the lower camp. They had reached the last half of what had been a new bottle of rye whisky.

'No need to report this at all, right, Mac?'

'Right, Vince. No need at all. 'Sides, who the hell knows?'

'I never saw the like of it, Mac. You have to look, really look, to find even a smell of oil.'

'Cleaned her right up, didn't they? Snow and all. They'll burn anything in them damned stoves, seal fat, lard, motor oil. It's a fact. I've seen them do it. Chucked a chunk of seal right into the firebox. Stink and smoke and them grinning and tee-heeing. But damn, there ain't much else to burn either.'

'I am personally most grateful for your timely assistance, MacGonigle, but it would be better that not much be said about this incident. Those Northern Affairs people…'

'Don't worry about me, Vince. Another drink and I'm going to have trouble remembering my name.'

Spring came with ducks and Arctic Tern squawking on the now

steamy, brown tundra. The warmer days had taken the snow, leaving gray rocks and blue ocean and white clouds. The beach road became Michael's evening walk and the site of the Inuit oil salvage was as gray and brown and desolate as the rest of a thousand miles of Arctic beach. You could hardly even see a smell of oil.

Chapter Eleven

For months, the cement mixer had been slowly sinking into the tundra by the side of the hangar, waiting for an empty flight west. The rusty beast was a self-contained unit comprising a four-cylinder gasoline engine, gas tank, rotating drum, support rack, and gear mechanism all mounted onto heavy duty rubber-tired wheels.

On Tuesday afternoon the word came down to move it. A civilian contractor building a warehouse at Cam Three had been assured that there was a cement mixer on location and now the man was upset, threatening all manner of rash things, such as charging the company overtime for men sitting around, if the cement mixer was not where it had been guaranteed to be. Or, to quote the head office fax from Colonel Nagy, 'The mixer will be in place yesterday or there will be action taken against the miscreant'.

Reactions were immediate. The Foxe Main American Air Force executive officer, warehouse lead hand, sector transportation officer, Foxe Main ground crew and all manner of would-be second-stringers got into the act. Nugent, the Foxe Main air traffic and cargo bum boy, made arrangements to have the oversized blender dispatched from his domain.

Two Inuit, 'Smiley' and 'Big Stoop', had been sleeping on the airport waiting-room benches since 0700 hours. They were not gung-ho for work. No, their availability was due to wives who had run them out with the immortal words so familiar to carefree husbands worldwide – 'Get out of here and find a job' – which resulted in their being available for hire. Nugent promised them twenty bucks if they would lend a hand with the loading of 'some miscellaneous hardware, out there by the hangar door and see Kelly when he gets here'. He promptly slammed his office window closed, thereby canceling any further discussion.

Kelly looked at the mixer and the available manpower and went in search of additional bodies that could be cut free from a coffee cup. When the work crew was finally assembled and the situation explained, the men stared at Kelly for a moment and then broke into hearty laughter.

'You're full of jokes this morning, Kelly.'

'Where'd you get this one?'

'Is this another Newfie joke?'

Smiley and Big Stoop muttered something about 'Maybe better go tea-time', but both knew they were stuck between the rock and the hard place, there being a hundred pounds of female wrath waiting at home. Kelly sent the two grunts for a forklift, block and tackle and some half-inch chain.

'And crow bars if you can find any.'

Kelly and the Inuit poked around the six-foot-square hunk of rusting machinery for a few minutes and then took a coffee break in Nugent's office.

Nugent asked, 'How long will it take to load, Kelly?'

'We'll have her on board by noon.'

'You sure?'

'Would I kid you? How much does it weigh?'

Nugent shook his head. 'I'll look it up. I think it will be around five tons.'

'Christ, you should have got a Hercules from the Trenton airbase.'

'Sure, Kelly, they send those things out like a Checker taxi.'

'Well it's not going to be easy, but when the boys get back what we'll do first is get it up on a flatbed truck. We can use the forklift for that, then, with a block and tackle we can roll her up through the cargo door and with another block and tackle skew her around the hatchway, a forward pull, and tie her down. Take about two hours. Right. Let's go, Smiley. Happy?'

The two Inuit grinned and nodded and said, 'Sure, boss. You got cigarette?'

The work went as Kelly had planned. The big, rust-splattered orange and white drum on wheels fought the five men every inch of the way, but muscle and steel prevailed and she was at last maneuvered into place.

Kelly left the tie-down to the Inuit and sent the bull labor back to their regular duties. In the office, Kelly and Nugent were back at the coffee.

'So, what does that piece of junk weigh?' Kelly asked.

'I'm calling it three tons. When it was delivered on the beach, the cargo manifest had it listed at five thousand pounds with accessories. I don't see no accessories so, say, three tons. Lots of margin.'

Nugent nodded his head. 'Ya, lots of margin.'

Kelly said, 'For that plane, it's a light load, but I wouldn't ride with it. Rattle, bang, bang, a man would be deaf as a post in the first hour. When does it leave?'

Nugent checked his wristwatch and said, 'The passenger should be here anytime now and then away we go.'

'There is a passenger. Who? Anyone I know?'

'Doc, Doc Rafferty, the Troppo tech.'

'Jeez, he won't go when he sees that thing.'

'He'll go. He's been trying to get to his new posting in instrument test and calibration at Cam Main for two weeks. He phoned this morning and when I told him about this flight he said, and I quote, "I am impressed. I was not aware that a cement mixer would warrant a private plane and I, a common technician, might be subject to extended delays and if I'm not on that flight…" then some ranting and I think our boy is getting borderline.' Nugent finished his coffee, smiled a self-righteous smirk and said, 'So, he insisted and I put him on.'

Kelly said, 'That Doc is usually a heads-up guy, but this time he may wish he'd kept his mouth shut.'

The bon voyage bottle was empty. Doc had finished the 'goodbyes and see yous' and at 1330 hours the Troppo truck deposited Doc and Doc's luggage at the airport Quonset hut and not a moment too soon. The pre-flight checks were finished and for the past ten minutes the flight crew had kept themselves busy practicing patience. Nugent had final say and it was 'No passenger no fly'.

Captain Donald Smale, ex-RCAF, would use the left-hand seat, and Burnett Duncan, ex-RCAF, would keep the co-pilot's seat warm. Mr. Duncan would be expected to occupy himself with observing the great skill with which the captain flew and it was hoped that he would overcome his awe and absorb some measure of the captain's delicate finesse.

An incidental duty would be seal watching. Don's last RCAF posting had been on the North Atlantic submarine patrol and that flying technique was an accomplished skill that, justifiably, he demonstrated to junior personnel when occasion permitted; flying twenty feet off the deck, that is.

The captain was able to maintain, to some degree, the skill of chopping wave tops with the propellers by chasing seals off the ice floes; a practice not condoned by Polar Aire but it certainly gave everybody else involved a thrill.

When Doc was escorted to his seat by the co-pilot he paid small heed to the vast load that filled so much of the DC-3's cargo area. All he wanted was a seat, a soft place to rest and recover. Doc was sore and aching. Tired of good old boys and good old booze.

'Just point her west, Burn. I'll be okay. Aaron is waiting at the other end, and… what the hell is that?'

'That's your personal Martini shaker, Doc. We put it on just for you.'

'Jeez, tourist class is getting ridiculous.'

'Doc, you booked the flight. Have a sleep and in two hours we'll drop this thing at Cam Three. Okay?'

Burnett made a prudent exit and the slamming of the cargo door was the signal for Captain Smale to begin the take-off. The twin-engined, blue-striped plane built up speed and gradually lifted towards the white puff clouds scattered in the sky above. At the desired altitude the benevolent captain nodded to his eager understudy and relinquished the command.

'How's the Doc doing?' he asked.

Burnett grinned and said, 'He looked like he was going to sleep for a week.'

'It must be another of his talents, sleep anywhere, anytime. He's a good man but don't play poker with him.'

'I take it you did?'

The captain settled himself comfortably, sighed and said, 'Ya,' and changed the subject. 'Take a look out there. Isn't that the greatest? Have you ever noticed how clear the skies are north of Sixty? I think… no, I know… it's the lack of smog. We never get any up here because the winds never blow out of the south. It's true. The winds blow from the west, the east and sometimes the north but never the south… so no smog.'

Burnett thought about it and said, 'Okay, but what about your

Atlantic tours? That must be clean air.'

'Not like this, Burn. Not like this.'

The sky beyond the shadows of the cockpit was of the texture that God left with man on the eighth day: sparkling whites and twenty shades of blue, a sky that picnickers dream of. Two thousand feet below, the shadow of the plane raced ahead, across intermittent ice floes and occasional small, black objects would detach themselves from the ice and disappear into the blue water.

'Seals taking an afternoon break,' the captain remarked. 'It's amazing how those things detect us at this distance.'

'It is remarkable. Do you think it's the shadow, or do they hear the engines?'

'Damned if I know, but I've seen them on their tails, almost standing up, noses pointing at the sky and when they get as high as possible, they swivel around, almost like a fat ballet dancer, then flip off the edge of the ice into the water. It's a very comical routine.'

'We've got lots of time. Let's see if there's anything for the Winnipeg Ballet Company down there.'

'You sure it'll be all right, Don?'

'No problem. Okay, I got it,' and the captain took the left-hand control column in hand. The plane's nose dropped below the horizon and the descent had hardly started when a loud yell from the cargo area momentarily froze both men.

'Jesus Christ, Don. You'd better level this plane off or this oversized slop pot is going to be up there with you.' Doc sounded wide-awake.

Doc had tried to sleep, but the cement mixer was parked two feet from his comfort zone. Groaning and squeaking, almost animal-like, the noise rose and fell as the machine complained about being tied in this fashion. Doc had tried a potion of magic from the eighty proof bottle and that had alleviated the smell of oil and gasoline, but did nothing for the ear-piercing squeaks and squeals. Doc had felt momentary relief when the mammoth chunk of junk, that was using so much of his travel quarters, began a slow, steady movement towards the thin, forward bulkhead.

Doc's yell alerted the professional pilot. Smale was trained and reacted; instantly, the plane was pulled up and flying level. The pilot said something to Burnett who hurried back for a look-see and found Doc kneeling beside his seat, peering under the machine.

'The wheel blocks have moved. Been pushed out of position.'

'You're kidding, Doc.'

The second officer came up with a flashlight and knelt beside Doc.

'There they are, against the port bulkhead.'

'That's them, but before we get them back in place we better tie this roll-around mother down.'

Doc made his way forward and spoke through the cabin doorway.

'Hold her steady, Don, she's slipped a few inches of her girdle but we'll have her fixed in a minute.'

The once taut, one-inch nylon rope that had fastened the machine's front end to a floor ringbolt, now drooped in listless uselessness. Doc undid the lashing and pulled up several inches of slack.

He called the pilot to tell him what was happening, and added, 'We had better check the ass end.'

In the shadows of the plane's tail, the once complete rope now sported two frayed ends and three spare feet of rope dangled beyond the knot. It would have to be enough. Doc and the co-pilot discussed the situation, finalizing a course of action.

'We'll get Don to start a gentle climb and just as this bitch starts rolling back we'll jam the wheel blocks home. Then with the front end locked down and this bucket of rust where she belongs we can splice that frayed rope on her ass.'

Doc and the co-pilot went about the business of securing the cargo and in a very short time the captain was called upon to begin making a gradual climb.

'Hold it, hold it right there. Good… steady. Damned good. Just another wrap and that will do it. Okay.'

Doc made his way forward for another small conference.

'Okay, Don. We've got the tail tied and I've got the front end guaranteed tight. When that rear rope parted, the wheel blocks slipped and there was nothing holding the ass except air. We jammed blocks under the wheels, but, to be sure everything is solid, will you start a gentle climb, then level off and then a gentle descent? Burn and I will be watching for any movement and we can pound the block tighter if we need to.'

'You sure those ropes will hold, Doc?'

'You can bet on it, now that we've got those blocks in place. That is one-inch nylon rope and you can lift ten tons with that stuff if it's a steady pull. The secret is a steady pull. Nylon rope doesn't work that well if it's jerked. It's a no-sweat situation, Don, this time she's tied down.'

The pilot complied with the temporary flight engineer's request and when the up/down maneuvers were completed, he was joined by the grinning grease-stained co-pilot and Doc.

The co-pilot said, 'That sucker won't move now, and Don, I won't mind if there's no more dancing seals.'

The captain said, 'Right. From now on, we check that geese are staying in formation. Okay? I think I owe you a case of whisky, Doc.'

'Make it a case of fresh milk and call it even.'

'Milk?'

'Yeah, I'm so fed up with that chalk and water mixture the cooks serve up, I could puke. Right now, I can't think of anything that would taste better than a glass of cold, creamy milk.'

The surprised-looking co-pilot said, 'That doesn't sound like a living legend.'

Doc answered, 'The trouble with this legend shit is that the legends are mostly human.'

The captain said, 'Anyway, a case of milk and thanks.'

One hour later, without further incident, the cement mixer was delivered to Cam Three and later that same afternoon Doc and Aaron were shaking hands at the Cam Main landing strip.

'Welcome to fun city, Doc.'

'Good to see you, kid.'

'How was the flight?'

'About the same. I still don't see how they keep those things in the air.'

Chapter Twelve

The bar at Cam Main was redecorated by three of the boys who were tired of the institutional austerity and they spent long, spare-time hours on the reconstruction. They skillfully hid sewer pipes, water mains, electrical wiring and fire alarm cables with a fabricated false ceiling. The use of indirect lighting in the corners and behind the bar added a dash of sophistication. The hi-fi and records were sheltered in a stylized imitation oak cabinet that was suggestive of a manor house's library wall. The chrome tubular furnishings were incongruous but the subdued illumination softened the full picture and did much to conceal small faults and signs of usage by more boisterous patrons. The refurbished area was conducive to relaxed conversation, at least, for the majority of the users.

Nelson Karver, the current week's appointed volunteer bartender sat glowering from a stool behind the bar, conversing with no one. The bartender was expected to remain in a relatively sober state and if Nelson had had his druthers he would be getting pissed to the eyeballs. DEW-lining was wearing a bit thin and Nelson, with five months of a first contract behind him, was wondering if the cramps he sometimes suffered were from a stomach disorder or sexual starvation.

Aaron drifted in at 2100 hours and greeted the dour Nelson with, 'Hey, buddy, Saturday night and you own a bar. What more can you want out of life?'

'Nothing, maybe a dame or two or three, but how about you, Aaron? You want a beer?'

'Sure. You got a Labatt's or maybe a Blue?'

'Nothing but Molson and with all the transients that have been stopping over, there ain't a hell of a lot of that.'

'We can get some from Yellowknife, but it will cost a bundle, coming air cargo. Talk to Carl and he can make the arrangements.'

Aaron joined a group of supply types and the site's 'J' mechanic and his arrival at their table interrupted a small argument.

'What do you think, Aaron?'

'About what?'

'About never meeting any Eskimos. About this business of staying away from them, that's what.'

This invective from Leo Pendergast surprised Aaron for it was the first time the overweight supply clerk had expressed an interest in anything except food, booze and money.

Leo continued. 'Before I came up here I heard all kinds of things about Eskimos, you know, things like them being great hunters and them Eskimos squaws being so friendly and look over there.' Pendergast waved his hand in the direction of blind Charlie. 'Look at the one Eskimo I've met.'

Aaron grinned and said, 'You can hardly take Charlie as typical, hell, most days you can't take Charlie.'

Charlie, hearing his name, chuckled and nodded in the direction of the speaker. The group at the table ignored him. Pendergast continued, 'So who *is* typical? I've been here four months and all I've seen is Charlie and some guy running a polisher up and down the hall. Where do they keep the dames? The way I heard it, all you had to do was rub noses with them and they get so hot and bothered they would be tearing your clothes off out there on a snow bank. So where are they?'

Aaron offered a mild protest.

'They are strong family units, Leo, so this business about an easy lay is bullshit. If you really want to meet some Eskimos, go to church on Sunday.'

'Hey, Aaron, I've been there, two weeks ago, the seven o'clock service. The priest was so busy shaking my hand and thanking me that when I got out, everyone had gone.'

Arnold, the supply type, said, 'Buy Charlie a beer. Maybe he'll take you home and introduce you to his mother.'

The small weather-scarred Inuit, upon hearing his name, laughed and nodded at the men. Every Saturday the blind man made his way, three miles across the open windblown tundra, to the site and when the Saturday night revelers heard Charlie's cane tap, tap, tapping in the hall, the remarks were invariably the same.

'The bastard made it again.'

"You could bet your life on him.'

'Charlie is a total party animal, right, Charlie?'

Charlie had ventured into the recreation area during the first-night celebrations of the remodeled bar's opening and was now as much a part of the Saturday night bash as the beer. The old hands acknowledged his presence by buying him an occasional beer and offering short, friendly greetings, such as, 'How are things looking tonight, old buddy?'

The 'Kabuna', white men from the south, were amazed by Charlie and his weekly pilgrimage. They admired his bravado and determination but were embarrassed that a blind person would endanger himself so recklessly for such a small thing as a can of beer. When the tribute had been paid, the can of beer placed in Charlie's open hands and the acknowledgment made, the gracious 'Kabuna' would discreetly retreat from Charlie's presence and with good reason.

New men who entered into the ritual of honoring the small Inuit soon discovered why he sat alone. He smelled. Charlie was not a fastidious person. There is no means by which to have a daily bath in an Inuit village and this fact of life became an obvious truth within Charlie's five feet of personal space. There was the obnoxious smell of seal oil, add a dash of soured cod liver oil perfume mixed with urine and the smell of the several hundred body parts, which was defiantly different to the odious scent of last week's cigarette butts and sour beer that prevailed in the bar space.

At times, after several beers and several trips down the hall to the toilet, Charlie would have the stuffed sofa and ten square feet of surrounding floor space all to himself. This ostracism did not bother Charlie. The reason for being here was the beer and there was no need to join the white man's conversation, in fact, as the evening progressed, he would shush those who would interrupt the conversations he was having with the spirit world; guttural monologue, some laughter about nothing obvious, a few unintelligible grunts and then some weird squeaky-voiced chants. This was Charlie's contribution to the Cam Main Saturday night bar. The regular party animals ignored him.

A lull in the room's conversation brought a half-hearted curse from Nelson.

'Somebody change that damned record. I've heard *Sentimental*

Journey three hundred and seventy times too often and I don't need anything about *Blowing in the Wind*. See if you can find that *Limelighter* record. Okay. Aaron, you ready for another?'

Pendergast ordered a beer and started telling Nelson about a manufacturing company.

'Hammond Nail company. They were having trouble with sales so they hired themselves a high-priced advertising company. When the new ad campaign was ready, the directors met in the boardroom where the ad man had a large easel covered with a velvet cloth.'

Somebody interrupted the story, needing more beer. By ten thirty things had picked up, but not much. The game of poker dice had been forsaken because the dice kept falling through a hole some klutz had burned in the bottom of the leather cup. No one wanted the bother of passing the one straight cue around the snooker table, and the dartboard was a mess.

At 2300 hours, the shift change, a few more guys wandered in and in the corner, Nelson Karver was telling a recent arrival about the Hammond Nail company.

'The guy pulls the velvet drapes and there is a picture of Jesus Christ hanging on the cross. The caption in flowery script reads, "They used Hammond nails". So, the directors send the guy away. "Not what we had in mind at all. Need a more civilized picture. Very crude. Not the Hammond Nail company." So, the guy leaves and a month later, he's back with another presentation.'

The story was interrupted by the night cook bringing in platters of deep-fried shrimps and cocktail sauce. The men swarmed the platters of food, everyone except blind Charlie and Nelson. Between sips of beer and mouthfuls of shrimp, the conversation about Inuit lifestyle continued.

'They were hunters and lived off the land. A few still do but more and more they settle down in a permanent place and live where there might be a job, housing and settlements.' This capsulized description of the northern nomads was offered by Brownie.

Ted 'Brownie' Brown was the resident northern expert, having spent ten years with the Canadian Department of Northern Affairs as a radio operator and four of those ten years had been here at Cambridge Bay. After a swallow of beer, Brownie continued.

'Ten years ago the Eskimo used this area for a summer camp, put up their tents, caught some fish, but come freeze-up they left. These days, the government issues a family allowance check every month and the wives want to stay and spend it. There's the school, the hospital and food all year at the Hudson Bay store. Some of the men still hunt, go out for a week, but hell, they've covered the same country so often it's a wonder when they bring home a rabbit. A few persistent ones head farther out, but they don't have the dog teams and can only go so far on the skidoo or all-terrain vehicle before they have to head back for gas.'

Brownie stopped for some beer and Arnold got started.

'Speaking about dogs, last Friday after chow, I started walking to the "Bay". Wanted to get some air as much as anything and I headed out, straight across the ice. I could see the store lights and walked towards them. I'd walked twenty minutes across the ice when I hear this real mean growl right in front of me. Well, I stopped breathing and then I started backing up slow. Damned if there isn't another growler behind me. I stop all movement and stand, trying to see. It's darker than hell out there.'

Someone quipped, 'You should have had Charlie's cane.'

Arnold continued. 'Yeah, about then I should have had the Mountie's gun. Anyway, I bent down, trying to see, and what I see was a mouthful of teeth a foot away, and the teeth are tied to a stake driven into the ice. When I look real hard I can see about twelve dogs. Spread around. Some were lying curled up, but most of them were standing, looking like they just heard the supper bell. I tell you I was some slow and easy getting out of there.'

Brownie said, 'You were lucky. It was likely hunters from another village who stayed overnight with some relatives. The dogs, being strangers, would have the village dogs raising all kinds of hell, so the hunters staked them out on the ice. Those Eskimo dogs are always starving so if just one had taken a piece out of you the whole pack would have pulled free and attacked, and you, buck-ho, would have been hamburger. It's rare to hear about strange dog teams nowadays. If the DNA (Department of Northern Affairs) learn of them they call in the Mounties. Right now.'

Pendergast asked, 'Why the Mounties?'

Brownie explained. 'Nobody is sure about rabies and the

Mounties have the power to enforce the Wild Dog Act. If they get called, they shoot a few and take some blood samples. They play safe and it's a sure way to control the dogs.'

'It sounds radical, Brownie.'

'Well, about a year ago at Cape Dyer, a guy was out for an evening walk. A cook named Shank ran into some dogs and they jumped him. They took him down and ripped a half-pound of meat off his ass and he bled to death before he could get back to the site. The next day the Mounties flew in and shot eleven dogs. Three tested rabies positive.'

Brownie paused to take possession of the last shrimp and Nelson yelled about closing.

'Come on, you guys, it's one o'clock for Christ's sake. Go to bed.'

The men sat quietly, absorbing the ugly picture. A radician was telling his buddy the Hammond Nail story.

'So the guy comes back with another presentation. Once again the directors assemble in the boardroom and once again the guy pulls open the velvet drapes and this time, Christ is crumpled up, lying at the bottom of the cross and the caption reads, "They should have used Hammond Nails".'

A small group sat smiling, enjoying the beer buzz. They finished the bottom of the cans and realized the bar was closed and Nelson Karver and the blind Inuit had left.

Aaron remarked, 'If Charlie's gone home, it must be late.'

'How does he do it, Aaron? How does he get around? Have you figured it out?'

'He told me he follows the sound of the diesel generators. He said he can hear them five miles away but he did admit it was tough when the wind blows.'

'What about when he's going home?'

'Charlie said he has an old dog at home who howls something terrible until Charlie is safe inside the house. Sounds weird but that's what he claims.'

'Do you believe it?'

Aaron thought for a moment and said, 'I do. Eskimos seem to have sharper senses, you know. They use their eyes and ears a hell of a lot more than we do and they notice all kinds of things we take for granted, like the generators. I don't hear them.'

Brownie said, 'You have that right. We subconsciously tune them out.'

Aaron continued, 'That's it. I'm not aware of the noise, and yet Joseph, the Eskimo janitor, said that one of them was running short of oil and sure as hell, it was. And this was before the powerhouse gang caught it. Real sharp ears, especially that Charlie. I think he could hear a mouse fart.'

Pendergast said, 'You know it would be interesting to meet, really meet, some of them – Eskimos, that is. Think what it would be like if you went to Australia and didn't see a kangaroo. Damn, I would hate to go home and have never seen anything except these four walls and twenty guys from Toronto.'

Aaron quipped, 'Talk to Raoul. He's from Montreal. Now there's a different language. He's almost like someone from another world.'

'Oh sure, but you know what I mean. These people, the Eskimos, they're different. A different culture and we'll never see it. And we're stuck on this damned site. There must be some way to meet them, talk to them.'

Aaron nodded his agreement and said, 'You could get a job with DNA, Department of Northern Affairs or maybe… I've got an idea. Tell you what. I'll see the boss tomorrow and check it out with him.'

Aaron met the sector superintendent as he was leaving the remains of his Sunday roast beef and Yorkshire pudding dinner.

The big man was in a jovial humor and he greeted Aaron with, 'Where you been? The only time I see you is after meals. You some kind of seagull?'

'How are you, Dave? Can you spare a minute?'

'Anytime, kid. What's it about?'

'Sometime ago, you were talking about a social club, that there should be something besides the Saturday night beer drinking. Get the technicians away from the Triple S Club bar.'

'By God, Aaron, we sure need something. About all that happens here are hangovers and gripes about the mail. What do you have in mind?'

'How about a bingo game?'

'Come on, Aaron. You can do better than that.'

'I know bingo doesn't sound like much, Dave, but there is a kicker.'

'Like what? By God, Aaron, I'm about ready to try anything. The morale around here is getting lower than a snake's belly and if there is a way of getting the men out and mixing… well, I'll try anything reasonable.'

'Dave, I admit that a bingo game won't be much, but some new faces, different people that we don't see every day.'

'You mean Eskimos?'

'Right. The men would be meeting someone new and it would be a change. The Eskimos would come. This being a white man thing. We could check with the priest and the government administrator. Invite them too.'

'Damn it, Aaron, you might have something here. I've been curious about these people myself. What kind of prizes do you have in mind? Would you charge admission?'

The two sat down and within an hour had the details worked out. Dave, the highest-ranking Federal Electric employee, would approach the village administrators for approval. Aaron would recruit some of the DEW-liners and with a little luck the pieces would be in place for the Cam Main 'Wednesday Night Bingo Game and Social Evening'. Dave agreed, but with reservations, to release three cases of beer to be opened only after the games were finished, and with the understanding that the bar would damned well be closed at 2300 hours.

'Aaron, this might be all right. New faces, different kind of party. Say, do you know if it's true about rubbing noses?'

'I don't know about that, Dave, but have you heard about the Hammond Nail company?'

On Wednesday evening the site was in an expectant mood, something like a new homeowner meeting the neighbors. Extra chairs were moved from the reading room, plywood sheets protected the pool tabletop and the bar area decor had been embellished with the addition of makeshift benches and odd tables. A public address system had been installed and at 1900 hours the bingo rooms were ready.

At 2100 hours a mixture of village people began to arrive. They paid a dollar at the door and found seats. The big surprise of the evening was blind Charlie who arrived in the company of his daughter and son-in-law. Introductions were made and Aaron found the Charlie party seats in the bar area. Aaron thought Charlie would be more comfortable there. It was after they were seated that he realized what was different about the blind Inuit. Charlie had bathed, his hair was trimmed, his clothes were clean, and he smelled of aftershave lotion.

'What happened to you, Charlie?'

'I'm sorry, Aaron. My daughter was embarrassed by my old clothes. I knew you would be disappointed, but she argued.'

'Me, disappointed? How?'

'I know the "Kabuna" expects the Eskimo to be hunters of seal and I have stayed as a hunter so that you would know me. I am sorry to have changed to a person of the village.'

Charlie's black-haired daughter added, 'It is true. When my father was first a guest here, someone argued with him. They said he was an imposter. He did not smell like a hunter of seals. My father is still proud of the days when he did hunt. He hopes that you will not forget what he was and that you will remember he is a true Eskimo.'

Aaron was emphatic.

'I will, I will never forget that Charlie is a true Eskimo. Charlie, you come just as you are. Okay?'

The first of the Wednesday night bingo games was a great success and the model for future social gatherings with the Cambridge Bay villagers. A great time was had by all. The natives were captivated by the game of numbers. The last game of the evening, a blackout, cleaned out all the door admission monies. The crowd sorted out parkas, mitts and kids and made a polite exit. Each Inuit stopped and thanked Dave, the 'Kabuna' chief, and assured him they would come back.

When the reading room, the pool table and the bar had been restored to normal, the entertainment committee assembled for debriefing and to claim the rewards. Karver, Pendergast and Simpson began setting out the free beer. The committee waited, and when everyone had been served, all stood, including blind Charlie, who had sent his daughter and son-in-law home. The standing men saluted the day's hero, Aaron.

The spokesman said, 'Not only do we get another social evening but we get beer. Here's to this giant amongst us.'

'Here, here.'

Blind Charlie added an explosive burp, and the assembly took note of his presence.

'Hey, is that Charlie? By God, men, lookee over here.'

'How are you, Charlie? What do you see tonight, buddy?'

'Say, Charlie, who was that doll you had out tonight?'

'Ya, Charlie. How about fixing me up?'

For the first time the men saw Charlie's total smile, an ear-to-ear look of pleasure.

Shortly after the first round, he called loudly, 'Aaron, Aaron, who is ready for beer? Come, this round I buy for my friends. Here, take the money I have here.'

Charlie waved several bills and Aaron did as the small Inuit asked. The men, Charlie included, sat and talked and, finally, the Inuit began bundling up in his parka and boots.

He said, 'Well, boys, I go now. Be here Saturday. Okay?'

'You bet, Charlie.'

'Take care,' and other warm comments followed the tap, tap, tapping down the hall.

The next night, Dave joined Aaron at dinner.

'How are you, boy? Say, did you hear? They called the Mounties in today?'

Aaron asked, 'Called them in? Who called them? I don't follow you, Dave.'

'The DNA. They had some trouble with a pack of dogs. There have been some dogs feeding at the town dump and last night, damned if they didn't go after some Eskimo.'

'Who was it?'

'The district director, I suppose. Oh, the Eskimo. I'm not sure. These Eskimo names don't mean much to me and when I was talking to the director… Say, he said he wanted to thank you for last night. Said it was thoroughly enjoyable.'

'The name, Dave, the Eskimo. Is he okay?'

'Oh, sure. I don't know about the name, something like Kapatinick or Cap-a-chine. I don't understand those damned names. Anyway, they flew her out to Frobisher this afternoon. She'll be all right. Lost a lot of blood but the Mounties cleaned up all the dogs around town so we won't have any worry about that. Anyway, about next week. I was thinking how we can speed those games up. What do you think of this?'

On Saturday night, at five minutes past 2000 hours, the familiar tap, tap, tap could be heard coming down the hall. Aaron met the blind Inuit and escorted him to the biggest chair.

'We heard about the dogs, Charlie.'

'Dogs all gone, Aaron. No problem. You having beer?'

'I'll get you one in a minute, but what about your dog? Did they shoot him?'

'My dog. What dog?'

'Jeez, Charlie. The dog that howls until you get home.'

'Aaron, I don't understand you. Charlie is a fine hunter. I need no dog. What can dog say to me? Besides who would feed dog? No, I have no dog. What kind of beer, Aaron? Maybe the Labatt's be nice. Okay?'

In the morning, Aaron checked the small mukluk tracks leaving the site. The footprints marched in a straight line towards the distant native settlement; a settlement which, incidentally, lay directly between the radar site and the Mountie barracks, four miles across the frozen Cambridge Bay. Aaron couldn't hear the throb of the eight-cylinder diesel generator but he could see the white exhaust plume, spiraling skywards in the minus-thirty-degree Arctic air.

Chapter Thirteen

The darkness of the Foxe Main radar room dissolved in a burst of white light from the suddenly opened door. The man in the swivel chair wheeled towards the offender; the half-mouthed curse was stopped when the visitor was recognized. The long shaft of light that had fragmented the blackness silhouetted the sector chief.

'Come in and close the door, Mr. Bradley. You're wiping out the radar screens' display.'

With the door closed the blackness was restored, relieved only by the two twenty-inch circles of soft white light sitting side by side in front of the operator at eye level. On each screen a bright line revolved and occasionally, as the wiper rotated, a burst of light smaller but brighter than a match flare bloomed. The bloom was the echo of the transmitted radar pulse and the usual target would be nothing more than a mundane flock of ducks flying through the antenna transmit path, but there were many hours when there would be no changes to the twin, glowing faces. The new arrival stood quietly, allowing eyes, which had been rendered blind, time to regain some degree of vision, but, shortly, he cautiously found and sat in a second swivel chair.

'Well, Michael. How are you? It's not often I have the time or the occasion to see the heart of this business.'

'Glad to have you, Mr. Bradley.'

'Call me Frank, Michael. Just Frank.'

'Okay. Frank it is. So what's new?'

'Well, hell boy, that's my line, but what I wanted to do was come over and thank you. Thank you personally for the great job you've done on the phones. Say, you mind if I smoke?'

A match flared before Michael could remark about the affect of smoking in an enlarged broom cupboard.

'Say, Michael, you're a new man in my sector, right?'

'Yes, sir. Five weeks. I came over from Cam One.'

'I heard about that, your trip on the ice. That was a good job you did there. How's Harry? Harry Edwards?'

'Okay when I left, sir.'

'It's Frank, call me Frank. I just saw last week's sector maintenance log. You're the tech who did the repairs to the switchboard and this is a personal thank you from the Foxe sector super himself. Those damned phones have been buzzing and clicking and half the time you wind up talking to the warehouse when you call the hangar or some other damned fool thing.'

'No sweat, Frank, but I used up all the spare parts. Nothing left in stores and we need to order in a barrel of components. This time we were lucky and had everything we needed but it could get serious without spares.'

'Okay, it's in the book. Spare parts for phones and I tell you, I'm damned-well glad to have working phones. It's been a year, maybe even two. No one in the sector knew dick about phones or switchboards. So tell me, Mike, where do they teach this? At one of the tech schools? One of the military electronic trades?'

'Not quite. We had the same switchboard in my home town and I used to tinker with it. Mrs. Jessup owned the telephone company and when her husband died, she let me fix this and that and—'

'That a fact? Well, by God, you're sure a good man to have here,' Frank continued. 'For two years I've been trying to get them pinheads in personnel to hire someone who can fix these telephones.'

'The strouger mechanic is a rare bird, Frank.'

The sector superintendent looked confused. 'Strouger?'

'That's the name of the relay system that goes clank, clank, clank back there in the mux room. It was the strouger switch that needed cleaning and repair.'

'Strouger. And we need more parts?'

'Right you are, Frank, if we can get them. This thing is a dinosaur. Nowadays they use stuff called crossbar – a form of electronic switching. Solid state, quick and quiet, uses less power.'

Frank said, 'Every week things get more complicated. Some days, Michael, I don't know if I'm on the same globe. Why, hell, the equipment on this site has been in service less than five years and every month I hear talk about another upgrade. Well, that's another matter. There is one thing that I want you to do. Drop by my room after dinner for a drink. Bill Frame will be there. I reckon you know him. Your boss, the communications super.'

'Sure, I know Bill.'

'Well, he'll be there and maybe a couple of others. We'll have a drink and I got another matter. A little proposition. So I'll see you about eight.'

'Thank you. I'll be there, sir, at 2000 hours.'

At 1955 hours, the five foot, nine inch, chunky young man strode down the long living-quarters hall. He stopped at the reception area counter to compare his wristwatch with the wall clock. He then spent two minutes browsing the bulletin board notices and at precisely 2000 hours he knocked on the door marked Number One. It was opened immediately by the six foot, gray-haired sector superintendent, who had dressed for the evening. Pearl button shirt, silver bolo tie, hand-tooled belt and two pounds of silver buckle. He had a glass of whisky in his hand and a long cigar sticking out of his tanned face.

'Come in, boy, come on in.'

'Hi, Frank, I'm not early?'

'Right on time. Say, you didn't have to get all dolled up.'

Michael, in sweater, slacks and black loafers, was a study in causal compared to the cowboy sector sup. Already seated was Bill Frame, who raised his half-full glass to Michael.

'How are you, Michael?'

'Bill.' Michael acknowledged the greeting and started into the room but was quickly restrained by Frank's hand on his arm.

'Jeez, take your shoes off. You get any freaking shoe polish on this rug and how in hell can I send it home?' Frank shook his head. 'Christ, this freaking skin cost eight boxes of beer and four hundred bucks.'

He backed Michael off the polar bear rug and after Michael slipped his loafers off he took a quick look at the furnishings. He had expected the sector superintendent's quarters to be more comfortable than the orange-painted metal bed, metal dresser and chrome tubular chair furnishings that were the standard DEW-line decoration. Being a reigning monarch, the superintendent was accorded slightly more. There was no visible bed. Instead, there were two club chairs, a sofa with coffee table, matching end tables, two tri-light lamps and a seascape oil painting on one wall. Carpet covered the floor area beyond the edges of the white bearskin rug.

'What will you have to drink, Michael?' Frank asked. 'How about some of this Southern Comfort.' He held up the bottle. 'Damn fine mountain dew.'

He handed Michael a half-full glass and said, 'There's ice in that barrel on the table. You know Vince?' He pointed to a third man who had a silver moustache and bow tie, and who in turn greeted Michael.

'Vince, how are you?'

'Fine, mighty fine. Grab a seat.'

This was prime stuff, for compared to the stark walls of Michael's accommodation, this was the penthouse suite.

Frank in a depreciating tone said, 'Not bad huh, boy? I had to use part of the room next door. Moved that wall four feet. We could put a real skinny guy in there, but I use it myself. Got my bed in there.'

'You've done a great job, Frank,' acknowledged Michael.

'Well, I needed a place to entertain the USAF generals, so I wound up with an army camp bed to sleep on. What the hell, we all have to suffer out in this wilderness. Right, Michael?' The sector superintendent continued, 'What I wanted to discuss was these switchboards; the phones, Michael, how about you taking over the sector phone system? Make it your baby. It would be a shame to let it go to hell again and I figured, or Bill and I figured, that you would be the best man. You should get together with Harlow Meadows in supply. Get the spare stock up to snuff, whatever you need to keep them bells ringing. Can you handle that, Michael? I'll get your promotion orders by TWX (teletype writer exchange) PDQ. Okay?'

'What about my duties as radician? The lead rad won't be happy filling my shift.'

Frank nodded to Bill Frame and said, 'That would be 'Fat Boy' Shockton, right? Bill here can deal with that. Right, Bill?'

Michael smiled and said, 'Sounds good. When do I start?'

The room filled with smoke and talk about the lack of mail.

Two days later, Michael presented thirty-eight pages of handwritten yellow and buff copies of the ANAF requisition form, number 56832-46463.04 to Harlow Meadows, the sector supply clerk.

'I need this yesterday, Harlow,' he said, pushing the forms across the counter.

'What the hell is it?' asked Harlow, looking down at the pile.

'Parts we need for switchboard repair and maintenance.'

'Jeez, you going to build a new one?'

'That's my minimum. When can I get them?'

The supply clerk was looking through the pages and muttering about, 'I'm going to have to check every frigging number.'

Michael explained. 'The parts' catalogue list is alphabetical, which screws up the number sequence. You don't have to check. It's all listed and the man himself said okay.'

'Ya, well thanks but I'll still have to check it.' Harlow sat shaking his head. 'Jeez, I'm going to need a coffee.'

With a noticeable lack of enthusiasm, Harlow began the monotonous routine of checking the fifteen hundred names and numbers and was halfway through the pile when a coffee spill across the desktop was partly blotted up by Michael's neatly penciled requisition forms. The penciled figures of the bottom page blurred but Harlow carried on, the coffee stain dried and eventually the stack was finished with the supply clerk's initial on each page.

The results of Harlow's productivity were added to an already full basket destined for the Com Center teletype operator. During the evening, telex traffic was at a minimum and it was during this quiet time that the massive parts order would be dispatched to head office in Paramus, New Jersey.

Paramus purchasing agents processed the substantial order with scarcely a raised eyebrow. The DEW-line required a lot of unusual items and the sum total of this order was not that far removed from the ordinary. The coffee-stained part numbers had been deciphered almost correctly by the Com Center operator. The order was placed with suppliers who could guarantee delivery in Montreal in time for the sea-lift. The blotted numbers were processed with the same dispatch. They were still ANAF item codes and the number groupings appeared correct. What the hell? If the world were a perfect place…

The sea-lift arrived, anchored and began offloading. Michael was called about some crates by the supervisor of supply. They had arrived with the sea-lift and were marked 'Attention: Michael Clow,

Federal Electric Company, Foxe Main, DEW-line Site, Hall Beach, NWT' (North-west Territories).

Michael worked for two days opening crates, checking invoices and stacking parts in storage bins in the correct sequence. At the back of the pile was something different. A larger case: the heavy timbered box bolted rather than nailed. He spent half a day of hard labor opening the crate and ripping off the heavy-duty overseas shipping material. Michael was alone when he stripped the last of the thick, brown, waxed covering from the Theatre Marquis popcorn cooker.

He checked and rechecked the invoice, dug through the pile of packaging material and it was, sure as Bob's your uncle, addressed to Michael Clow, Federal Electric Company, Foxe Main, DEW-line Site, Hall Beach, North-west Territories.

The ANAF part number agreed with the bill of lading and the shipping invoice, and the item in question had been included on the in-transit insurance policy. The crate and contents were consigned to him. Michael was now the proud owner–operator of a 'Super Tastee' hot-buttered popcorn machine. PLEASE READ ENCLOSED INSTRUCTIONS BEFORE USE.

Michael pushed the colored plastic and chrome machine into the corner, muttering, 'What the hell am I supposed to do about butter?'

By October, the 'stay over' winter population had dug in, suffered the first freeze and penciled in the winter lifestyle appointments. The bridge foursomes were arranged, the snooker schedule was posted and, at the native settlement, the youngest children had gone south to school. Hunters were out doing their trap-line stuff, wives were at the kitchen stoves and the 'hanging-around-the-place' husbands had begun staring at the walls with blank looks.

The village priest, Father Clancy, was busy waging war on the evils that beset idle hands. The priest scurried and hurried from duty to duty and at times it looked like idleness was a runaway winner. The lines of battle had been drawn and the lean-limbed priest gathered his combatants round. The most depressing segment, the most visibly unemployed, were the youth: those twenty teenage Inuit with no work, no entertainment, nowhere to go, nothing to do.

Father Clancy's answer was a Youth Center – a place to hang out;

somewhere that a guy could rap with the buddies. The Foxe basin's cooperative fish shed had been empty for eight years but there was still a roof, doors, and weatherproofing which would provide Father Clancy's coterie, work for a great many days. The Youth Center Action salvaged an abandoned boiler and the wintry freeze was dispelled. The gloom was relieved with the addition of several arc lights that had been rescued from don't ask where. The Department of Northern Affairs and Natural Resources contributed fourteen rolls of roofing felt.

Mid-November saw the cycle of solvent and gasoline abuse being 'left off', which showed that knowing others were there, that others cared, they were helping themselves. The idle youth had found a hospice, a place to escape the elders' critical eye.

One afternoon Marjorie Tukai showed up with her guitar and where Marjorie went, Billy Papigatok and fiddle went. Simon, as always, provided some rhythm with a foot-stomping board and a snare drum. The music they played was popular and they were often accompanied with impromptu vocalizations from anyone in attendance. One afternoon old Edgar arrived with his accordion and the group began to sound pretty good.

In December, hand-printed posters announcing a Christmas concert were tacked to various walls and to the marching trees of the north: the village power poles. Two of the notices were posted on the DEW-line site bulletin boards. Tentative plans were made and there was some discussion about who was working, when.

At the fish shed, red and green crêpe paper streamers were strung from corner to corner with tissue paper rosettes tacked here and there in random fashion and there was silver paper and candles and the place looked like a party.

On concert night a row of tables served as the refreshment area – soft drinks, black tea or coffee. The Inuit rhythm group were sockeroo. They opened with some Hank Snow stuff, a couple of Lefty Frissel goodies and Marjorie brought the house down with *Shiny Bubbles*. The lineup at the refreshment counter spilled on to the dance area and the demand for 'Super Tastee' hot-buttered popcorn never ceased. The machine ran flat out all evening. Popcorn, in cups, in bowls or, when necessity dictated, by the handful. 'Super Tastee' was the pièce de résistance of the great inaugural Hall Beach social evening.

Chapter Fourteen

The lads were Resting and Restoring on the sands of the French island of Tahiti when Michael first voiced his lament to Jake about his switchboard duties at Foxe.

'It's fifteen months that I've been nursing that box of bolts and I tell you, I'm ready to pack it in.'

'Sure, Mike, I know what you mean. But from what I hear, you have it pretty good.'

'It's a bummer, Jake. That board should have been replaced with a crossbar ten years ago.'

'It wasn't built ten years ago.'

'So what? It's a piece of garbage and they've made me the garbage man and now I want off the garbage truck.'

Jake thought a moment and then said, 'Tell Bradley or, better still, take a couple of bottles in for Carl. Carl can make the fix when all else fails. I think Mr. Brewster could arrange for your girlfriend to come in as the mail clerk.'

'Sure, Jake,' Michael agreed, 'that's what they say. Carl "Fix-it" Brewster. I'll try him. Just maybe.'

The following week, when the holiday kids started the Monday morning reprocessing at Winnipeg's Hangar Nine, a surprise was waiting. The Carrier tech positions at Pin, Cam and Foxe Main had been phased out; no more switchboard mechanics.

Michael was offered a choice of a transfer to Pin Three, where Carrier techs would continue, or he could take a radician post at an Auxiliary site.

Michael poured Carl drinks during the Cam Main lay over. The primary discussion was about the boredom of life on the Aux site. They were carbon copies, each was exactly the same: the diesel generators in the first four modules and living quarters at the opposite end; electronic equipment modules; the recreation and dining-room facilities in the center of the train on stilts to nowhere.

Carl expounded their merits and compared them to the melancholy place the 'I' (intermediate) sites had been.

'Those intermediate sites were breeding fruit cakes, loose screws and various certified dementia patients faster than personnel could find replacements. It was getting worse than California and you've heard about that?'

Michael shook his head.

'No. I don't think so.'

'Like packaged breakfast food, all flakes, nuts and fruits. Can you imagine five men locked up in a small three-room house for six-monthly periods. Anyway, they were phased out.'

'When did they close them?'

'About four years ago. What the hell, Michael, you can enjoy life out there. Thirty, forty guys, a variety of interests, some new hobbies. Call me for anything. Anything at all. Let me know.'

From the oval-shaped aircraft window at three thousand feet, the Arctic radar site looked deserted. Buttressed on two sides by the large drive-in screens, the long aluminum-sided building had been parked at the end of the railroad line and now needed an engine driver. Smaller buildings were scattered at random on the edges and a single vehicle track led away to the landing strip and hangar. The drive-in screens were microwave antennas; two pointing east and two pointing west. The smaller buildings included a warehouse, garage, temporary sleeping quarters for summer workers and an emergency shelter for use if everything else burned down.

The view south was the flat Arctic Ocean and the views north, east and west were miles and miles of treeless tundra. Here, thirty men lived and worked six-month-long tours and at the end of that time the technicians, mechanics or kitchen staff were free to fly south with bags of money and a giant-sized lusting for life.

In the summer, the sun never disappeared and in winter, it shrank to a two-hour red glow in the blackness beyond the broken ice. The day shift began life at 0600 hours with a shave, shower and nonchalant straightening of bed and room. The assigned bed-sitting rooms were twelve by fourteen feet and the men could arrange the bed, dresser and chair in any configuration desired if nothing protruded into the hallway.

The assistant cook would serve breakfast until seven thirty. All meals were cafeteria style and, depending on the cook, could be damned good or something else. The dining room was the social center where the men met for tea, coffee and conversation. The work patterns were singular activities and the two-man teams switched locations at break-time to defeat the monotony.

There were thirty-six chairs in the cafeteria with six men to a table. The seating arrangements were as clearly defined as those established in the court of Saint James – station chief, lead rad, and 'J' mechanic at the head table, with occasional guests, and furthest from the coffee pot, the grunts and greenhorns.

Because of the limited social contacts it was in the dining area where conversations were prolific. Here the men coming off the radar console would discuss problems or things left unattended at the shift change. The men on days off, the men on evening and midnight shifts would drift in and out for coffee and conversation during the day.

Planes were scheduled weekly. They took out the men who had completed the six-month tour and they brought replacement bodies, groceries, spare parts and mail. No one was immune to mail call anticipation. Great was the gloom if the mail was twenty-four hours tardy. A forty-eight-hour delay would cause surliness between friends and a week's delay… well, the less said the better.

At the Auxiliary site, the mail was sorted by the station chief, or his designated authority. He performed this duty by opening the mail sacks and dumping the contents on the change-room floor. He then retrieved the official mail, that mail pertaining to station affairs such as invoices for the laundry and groceries and the 'householder only' communiqués.

The Crypto mail was hand-delivered by the pilot and then the various envelopes, home town papers and subscription magazines were sorted and assigned to designated pigeonholes. Parcels and bundles were left scattered on the floor for the owners to retrieve. The men arrived in ones and twos to claim their mail and within the hour the change-room floor was picked bare except for the *Christian Science Monitor* and that would be gone the next day.

After mail call, the next most important item was the week's two movies. The movies were moved along the line from station to station with appropriate criticism being forwarded prior to a film's arrival by means of the radio service channel. A packed house was guaranteed when the preceding critique of the artistic epic would announce several frames had been dedicated to bare boobs or exposure of frilly under things. The movies were shown in the appointed social area – a section in mid-train used only on the occasion of the bi-weekly movies and the Saturday night bar.

Dinner was the main meal. A choice of entrées, varied vegetables with cheese sauces and fresh, hot rolls. A civilized affair. Lunch was a small event for very few of the men would bother with lunch. There was a strong belief that skipping lunch would keep the weight down, but most of the men would eat five snacks at the coffee breaks. There were always cookies, cakes, scones or pies and the cooks kept busy, stirring, mixing and baking, in the belief that staying busy, they would stay sober. Well, everybody has a dream.

In general, typical Auxiliary site life was a comfortable routine, and it was at a typical site that 'Dutch', a four-month greenhorn flipped. Went over the edge, foregoing his bonus and future considerations. The six foot, two hundred pound, fair-haired man from Germany blew his cool at the Foxe Two Saturday night bar and it was the lousy beer that did it.

The American military operating instructions made provision for a weekly beer ration of six cans per man. The decree was rigidly adhered to by the conscientious station chiefs because if they didn't they could get fired. Once a year the beer arrived with the sea-lift and at the end of eleven months the stuff would gag a thirsty camel. The fact that the beverage had turned milky white was no deterrent for those with a serious beer thirst.

Dutch began his Saturday night at 1330 hours with a bottle of illicit Kirshwasser, which may have been mailed by his mother. The pooling of the beer ration was a long-established Saturday night routine and those who would consume the stuff could ingest it in a civilized manner in the rec room. The station bar opened at 2000 hours and at 2300 hours, the weekly ration was finished. The Dutchman had devoured his six and processed an additional eight, which was no small accomplishment considering how poorly the stuff aged. When the beer ran out he paid the assistant cook fifty bucks for two bottles of cooking sherry and began some 'serious' drinking.

At one o'clock on Sunday morning a sentimental urge overcame him but when he was unable to arrange a phone connection with the south, he began making a terrible racket. The station chief arrived and tried to establish some measure of peace and quiet, but the Dutchman would not be reasonable. Indeed, in full voice, he suggested that the station chief do to himself some physically impossible exercises. Instead, the old spoilsport arranged Dutch's ticket south.

The big surprise, to those who knew him, was that the Dutchman had lasted as long as he had. Those studs who had been with the man at Streator, during the training days, would have bet several big ones that the Dutchman would have washed out in a month.

With the rest of his class, he had done his drinking at Rokies Bar and he was the only Federal employee who had made it with the blonde, bump and grind try-hard singer, called 'Bitsy'. Bitsy would never cause Doris Day unemployment but she could have given Jane Mansfield some anxious moments. Dutch was the only clown at Rokies Bar who Bitsy would sit and drink with.

An explanation was demanded of the Dutchman and he lied through his teeth and said, 'Bitsy and I have rooms on the same floor at the Tilton Hilton, in fact, they are, what do you say...? Adjoining, in fact, they are so adjoining that we share the same bathing facilities. It has become Bitsy's occasional request that I wash her back and that is all there is to it. No, no, no. I am happily married to Gretchen and Bitsy is very aware of this and why should I not help this poor lonesome girl?' It was a masterful performance and it was on the strength of such outrageous bullshit that the smart money had him down as a short-timer.

And so it was that the returning party-time kid, Michael Clow, newly declassified switchboard mechanic, was promoted and bundled post-haste to Foxe Two. Michael arrived in time for Monday lunch with a hand-carried personal dossier to be delivered immediately upon arrival to the station chief, Wimpy Luscar.

Wimpy was an ex-San Francisco public transit official. His

application form for Federal Electric employment noted this as his personnel office manager period. It was in fact his 'drive a streetcar' experience. He had demanded of the sector sup that the replacement tech be of a more temperate personality than that of the departing Dutch. His demands were partially met. Michael was not about to wrap his insides around a bottle of cooking sherry.

During the first month Michael finished a paint by number kit, taped forty-six of the Foxe One long-play records and in March he entered the station's Monopoly playoff. He roared into the month of April building model airplanes.

Michael and a radician named Dawson Pender plotted arrangements for the ice-fishing party during the Saturday night bar when some of the better tall tales were being retold, including Dawson's improbable account of a forty-pound lake trout taken from a nearby lake, using a ten-pound test line.

Izaak Ingakik, the Inuit truck driver, volunteered as guide, and Leo, the site mechanic, got into the act and offered a tracked vehicle from the motor pool. Izaak suggested that Norah, his happy little wife, and Dorothy, his seven-year-old daughter, would be a help in drilling the fishing holes.

'Hey, they would be good company.'

The newly formed Foxe Two Rod and Tackle Club left off consuming the eight-month-old tinned beer and went to talk George, the cook, into making up a picnic lunch. George agreed, but only after he was guaranteed a seat on the tracked vehicle.

In the morning, the fishing party gathered at the garage and Leo was emphatic.

'It is I, Leo Lapointe, who is in charge.'

The assertion was greeted with some derision by members of the party who noted that the zipper of Leo's fly was open. Leo busied himself with checking the oil and polishing the windshield, taking the responsibility of tour guide most seriously. The tracked vehicle, a bombardier (so named after its Canadian inventor, J.A. Bombardier), was equipped with two jump seats in front and two bench seats at the rear. The seven passenger seats were soon occupied. Dawson and Izaak had claimed space and were occupied with sucking up beer.

George had arrived and was handing the diminutive Norah

thermos flasks of coffee and boxes of sandwiches. He began making noises about, 'Where the hell am I supposed to ride? On the roof, maybe?'

Dawson proposed that Norah sit on his or somebody's lap.

'What the hell?' Leo fumed and grumbled. 'Nobody said nothing about the whole damned site coming.'

Norah crawled over some knees and joined the beer drinkers. With a snorting lurch, the yellow and black machine maneuvered across the graveled parking lot and headed out, towards the sun, which had recently appeared over the tops of the low, distant hills. The four-mile trip across the patches of open tundra and snowdrifts was accomplished without incident.

Conversation was at a minimum because of the engine noise and there was some resentment about Leo's pomposity. Dawson began a narrative about a French-Canadian taxi driver. 'He was granted three wishes. The first wish was that he be able to steer a car in a straight line and the second was…' The rest of the story was lost in the roar of the tracked vehicle being driven by an irate Leo.

The three-foot-thick layer of ice covering the lake had been blown free of snow and after consultation with Izaak, it was decided to drill the fishing hole at the mouth of a two-mile river that ran from the lake to the ocean. Izaak contended that the char would be schooling in this area, waiting for an ocean feeding. Leo disagreed. He drank a beer and made disparaging remarks about the location, the time of day and the way the hole was being drilled.

The remainder of the party sorted out lines and hooks. The warm Arctic-issue parkas were undone and then removed. At 1000 hours, the drill dropped through up to the handle and the fishing hole was ready. Norah was accorded the honor of the first hook, and then Dorothy. Space around the hole was parceled out and when the eight lines were in, it became apparent that a second hole was almost a necessity. About then, Norah jerked on her thin monofilm line and began hauling in the slender glistening thread, hand over hand. The fish came out in a tangle of lines and Red Devil hooks. Leo snorted and began to speak his native tongue, but then switched to English.

'What I say all along? I go where there is room to catch fish.'

A number of loud free-spoken thoughts were voiced but Leo was the loudest and ended the discourse with a demand for assistance from someone who was also skilled in the use of the ice drill.

'Not Izaak. No. No. Izaak will have to stay here. *Sacré bleu*, what if the bear approaches? *Mon Dieu*.'

The reference to the bear was to remind all those present that Leo had been the passenger on the *Arctic Rose* who had first spotted a polar bear on the ice. The fact that the sighting had occurred fifty miles west and had been eleven months ago did not deter the French-Canadian Davy Crockett. Once again, he loudly advertised his prowess of hunting, his keenness of eye.

'*Mais oui*?'

Dawson reluctantly succumbed to Leo's verbiage and climbed into the machine and away they went. The yellow tracked vehicle stopped midway between the fishing party and the ridge of ragged ice that marked the ocean shoreline. Two figures could be seen walking back and forth, obviously in disagreement, Leo stamping his foot much like a small child but that was probably an unkind observation for more likely he was testing the ice thickness by methods known only to the great Arctic hunters.

Three more fish were caught and the other fish in the lake went elsewhere. The lines were jinked with the small up and down wrist motions that Norah had taught. Cigarettes were lit. George opened some beer and passed it around. Scotty, a radician who had recently arrived back from R and R, was waxing lyrically about the merits of a Mustang car.

'A new concept. An American-built sports car.'

He had rented one whilst in Toronto and he wasn't sure but he thought he might still be paying the rent on not one, but two of them. There was no time to return the Toronto car when he had flown to Vegas. He claimed that omission was caused by the trouble he had in finding the Hertz agency at Pearson Airport, but the same thing had happened in Vegas.

'I haven't had a bill yet. There was a hell of a rush that was not of my doing. I was helping a harried chick. She had been unexpectedly called back to work during our get-acquainted period. I got lucky and for an extra twenty I got a seat on her flight, which incidentally was bound for Los Angeles, and which went by way of Vegas where she, the young lady, suffered a two-day layover. However, the plane stopped in Salt Lake, but that's another story.'

Scotty missed the return flight which was the fault of the leggy red-haired dancer he had met at the Tropicana. She was escorting him on a detailed tour of the vibrant nightspots.

'You would think that a girl in her profession would know the airline schedules.'

To cut a long story short, Scotty couldn't find which parking lot the Mustang was in and he was trying to make connections for Winnipeg in time for the Monday morning check-in.

'What the hell. I can replace one of them for twenty-five hundred.'

'The girl or the car?'

Scotty ignored the questioner.

George had brought the site's recreational archery set and a target was set up a hundred feet from the hole. Scotty, George and Dorothy made like Robin Hood and Maid Marian. Maid Marian proved the most skilful and then sandwiches, beer and pop were started on and another fish was pulled, flopping, on the ice.

The small occasional cloud came and went in the high, blue sky. Someone said something about getting back and 'What the hell is with that Leo?'

By 1400 hours the party was getting to be a drag. The beer was finished, the bow and arrows had been set aside and the group sat around the fishing hole, jinking the lines in an apathetic fashion. Two more fish were caught but neither was noteworthy.

Scotty voiced the group's opinion with, 'I'll bet that son of a bitch is laughing his head off. Thinks it's some kind of a joke. Us sitting here.'

It was another half an hour before puffs of black smoke were seen popping out of the distant bombardier and then the tracked vehicle made its way across the blue and white ice, stopping beside the men who were gathering up fishing lines and picnic gear.

Dawson got out of the passenger door and helped, while Leo sat in brooding silence, both hands gripping the steering wheel and staring straight ahead.

'How did it go, Dawson? Where's the biggest fish in the lake?' Michael asked.

Dawson didn't vocalize an answer but a big smile and a jerk of his index finger at Leo clued the men. The boys helped Dorothy and the still-smiling Norah into the back seats and after a short rooting around under the seats, two picnic beers, missed by Dawson or Leo, were opened and passed around. The fishermen from the distant ice hole were pushed for details. Leo, with a 'you can go to hell' attitude, kept his silence, hunching further around the steering wheel and the noise of the moving machine distorted Dawson's reply.

In the distance, the towering black Troppo antennas stood high in sharp relief against the white, rolling tundra and in the rattling bombardier the men sat swathed in Arctic clothing and small smiles. At the site Leo drove directly to the four-door truck garage.

George clambered out of the passenger seat and the rest of the party followed. Everybody was unloading and sorting. Dawson and Michael were talking when Michael's raised voice stopped the action. Everyone crowded around, even Leo who had been fiddling with an obscure problem at the driver's door. In an even louder voice Michael repeated the question.

'*Gravel*, all gravel?'

'Right,' Dawson affirmed. 'Leo was so damned sure the river made a bend, so, even though we were able to see where it ran into the ocean, he wouldn't drill anywhere but right there. I was so damned mad I went along with him and then he sat on his ass whilst I drilled two holes. Not one, but two, and both over four feet and I hit gravel both times. And the last time he had the audacity to say, 'What makes you pick this place to fish?'

Leo made a strong protest.

'No, no. That was the good place. It is the weight of the ice. It has pushed all the water out. You will see in the summer. It is there that I, Leo Lapointe, will catch the most fish of anyone.'

Chapter Fifteen

Seventeen Inuit waited patiently at the Lady Franklin Point airstrip. It was mid-August and the riotously colored flowers of the northern summer were now shades of brown. It was late in the afternoon and the sun was dropping into the western sea. Twenty feet above the gathering, the red windsock drooped listlessly on a white pole. The fur-trimmed blue parkas of the men and children and the brightly colored coverings of the women were a miniature carnival, a vivid contrast with the browns and blacks of the tundra background.

The silver plane came from the east and with no turns or changes in heading flew directly at the long, straight landing strip. A black dot that changed to silver and blue as it dropped towards the far end of the runway, touching down with small spurts of dust and then with nose high, rolled towards the waiting splotchs of color. It accomplished a short circle in front of the standing people and when it was positioned for immediate take-off the two circles of distorted air in front of the wings resolved into slow-turning propellers.

In the degree of quiet, a child's small voice could be heard now that the engine noise was muted. The plane had been chartered by the Department of Northern Affairs to deliver the young Inuit to and from school, a twice-yearly school bus. After twelve small airfields and a dozen stop-and-go pickups, twenty small, black-haired, wide-eyed, parka-clad Inuit would be deposited at Yellowknife in which they would suffer the ordeals of the white man's regimentation in the dormitories and cafeteria, learning rules that would govern their lives. Learning the Kalunait ways, the Kalunait books, laws and church. And then, when the geese returned to the summer nesting sites, the children would be returned to the remote fishing camps.

The large door at the back of the plane clanged open and aluminum steps were trundled into a position for passenger access. Two faces appeared in the blackness of the interior and one moved out and down the steps, a young woman in a blue uniform. Blue slacks, blue parka, blue cap. Her badge of authority, a Polar Aire stewardess.

She joined the group at the windsock pole and began a dominating monologue during which all the heads bent forward, watching and listening. She paused briefly to check the hand-carried clipboard and then with a stern face marched up the steps to the blackness of the open doorway. Four of the Inuit struggled after her, two small ones with bulky suitcases that dragged in the gravel and two adults burdened with rope-tied bundles.

The four disappeared into the blackness and shortly afterwards two small, wide-eyed faces were seen looking from the airplane windows. The Inuit bon voyage party smiled and waved and the two who had assisted the children rejoined the hand wavers. The curved door banged closed, the engine roar increased, and the propeller blades dissipated into white circles. The plane rolled forward, gaining speed and in a very short interval, blue sea and blue sky could be seen beneath the black dots that were the landing wheels. The plane climbed steadily away from the waving people, circled west and presently was nothing more than a dark spot in the washed-blue western sky.

Pete and Jerry Quinggoq were away to the winter school in Yellowknife. The winter interlude had been arranged by the district manager of Inuit Affairs at the time of the geese returning. Before the family moved into the summer tents a white man had explained the law about children and school. The family had gone into Cambridge Bay for summer provisions and it was there that the district administrator had expounded on the need for reading and writing skills. He had explained in great detail the white man's church and schools and how important books were. He informed the family that room for Pete and Jerry had been reserved in the Yellowknife school that coming winter. It was arranged that the family would meet the 'children plane' at the Lady Franklin airstrip, Lady Franklin being the closest airfield to the family's summer fishing camp.

The boys were resigned to being separated from their parents, uncles and aunts for the time required to ingest the white man's skills in reading and writing. They were unhappy about being taken from the hunting of seals but they were too young to have been active participants. The manhood adventures of their fathers would have to wait.

'Ai, perhaps this thing in distant lands will not be too bad.'

Seven times Pete and Jerry walked up the steps of the children's plane but, in the autumn that they were fourteen, they rebelled. During the sleep time they left the riverside camp, by the fish trap, and were gone for eight days.

They had no trouble in living off the land during those last warm days of summer. They had fish hooks and a rusted .22 rifle and there were berries and the living was very good. They returned to the family with some shame, knowing that they had caused their parents embarrassment before the white people, but there was also pride, for they had lived as hunters. They spent a month doing the work of women because they must suffer some humility, but their fathers were pleased with them and their mothers made them new mukluks. When the time of the walrus came the boys went in the big clumsy umiak, the family boat, and so joined the hunt.

By spring the awkward teens had filled out and changed from slight boys to muscled young men. Notwithstanding, in September, Jerry and Pete and their families again stood under the windsock at the Lady Franklin Point airstrip.

That winter the boys discovered girls and whisky and dormitory life became sufferable. In the white man's school they progressed to the study of woodworking, a curious vocation for the natives of a treeless land. They found great joy in cowboy music and discovered an aptitude for the fiddle and the guitar and then, with primary school finished, the boys returned to the land of their people where they were expected to hunt and fish and eventually take wives – as they traveled the road to manhood.

During June, in the southern port of Vancouver, the dockyards were busy loading an armada of ships. For several weeks cranes lowered tons of supplies into waiting ships and when these ships were full the hatches were covered and the ships were rigged for foul weather. Arctic weather to be precise. When the cargo master was satisfied that all was secure, the ships cast off and sailed the inland passage, past Prince Rupert, through the Aleutian chain and into the Arctic Ocean.

In September, the squadron of supply ships arrived in

Cambridge Bay and dropped anchor during the night. Men going and coming, enacting pre-breakfast rituals, deviating from daily patterns to crowd the seaward windows and study the strange clusters of light that twinkled in the before-dawn light.

By 0700 hours the first of the Second World War beach landing craft loading ramps were clanging open on the gravel beach. After a short interval the ten-ton Mac trucks, parked on the beach, roared into life, and began moving stacks of wooden crates and mounds of hundred-pound sacks up the dirt road to the vast empty warehouses. The level of noise grew, becoming a continuous roar as more and more trucks joined the round-trip procession and the clean air was lost to dust and black exhaust fumes.

In the blue waters of Cambridge Bay, the feature attraction was the *John McDonald*, the *Queen Mary* of the Arctic fleet. She had sailed from Vancouver in late June, had anchored in Prince Rupert to top up her fuel and had then steamed steadily up and around Alaska. From the Beaufort Sea she plowed into the ice-choked Amundsen Gulf and then into the shallow Coronation Gulf and finally here to Cambridge Bay. Old timers thought of the *John McDonald* as their personal beer-delivery wagon. A deliverance of greater import than mail. Last year's suds had not aged well, had turned and were now a milky white color. Not recommended for human consumption, so to speak. An indication of how far quality had deteriorated was the fact that three cooks had declined the weekly six-can ration.

In September, the high Arctic afternoons were cool and, by 1500 hours, the sun was starting its plunge into the gray waters at the western edge of the world. On the day of the *John McDonald* convoy's arrival, Jake Covlin finished his afternoon console duty, grabbed the air force-issue parka and started for the beach. The supply ships had been offloading nonstop for eight hours. Commands, queries and chatter between ships, beach and warehouses had poured from the console's mobile radio monitor throughout the day.

Jake joined a dozen others on the one-mile walk between site and beach and the normally hushed tranquility had been replaced by the sound of heavy equipment. The peaceful solitude was torn with the roar of diesels, the rattle of chain and the submerged, constant chug-chug of the big diesel-driven fuel pump moving aviation gas and diesel fuel from the offshore tankers to the silver beach tanks.

Jake made his way through the business on the beach, pausing on occasion to gawk. Eventually he arrived at the end of the gravel-filled concrete pier that screeched fifty yards into the ice-blue water and offered a panoramic view. Half a mile around the shore, to Jake's left, lay the settlement of Cambridge Bay, a montage of reds, blues, greens and whites, clustered, for protection, in the shadows of the two-story Hudson Bay store. Two miles farther, the Mounties' radio tower stood orange and white between brown tundra and blue sky.

Out on the water, in the center of the bay, five ocean-going vessels squatted in the flat, calm water. A long, white fuel line arched between a low-floating tanker and the shore. Three barges plied the waters between the fleet and the shore and on the beach, men driving spider-quick forklifts stacked crates and loaded trucks. Men, with clipboards in hand and hard hats on head, directed traffic. Beyond the work zone, on the high ground above the beach, a crowd of the village people fulfilled the non-paying job of shore-side supervisors.

On the left side of the dock, away from the frenzy, two slight Inuit worked on a small white motorboat beached on the gravel. It was a new boat. Delivered that day, and the proud owners were hard at work fitting an outboard engine to the modest area of the stern. With ear-to-ear grins they acknowledged Jake's warm greeting.

'Hi, Jerry. How are ya, Pete?'

The activities in the harbor commanded Jake's primary attention. The large *John McDonald* cranes were offloading piled-high pallets onto bobbing LCDs (landing craft defense). In one smooth arc, the skilled crane operator lifted, swung and placed the swaying load from mother ship to the deck of the bobbing water beetle that hovered alongside. Time after time without pause. Jake's studied observance of this performance was interrupted by the noisy racket of the Inuit starting the outboard. Jake knew the boys. They had met at the DOT Saturday night social. A community get-together, singsong and midnight lunch, and there had been further meetings and passing hellos at the Hudson Bay tobacco counter.

Jerry and Pete were cousins who had finished at the Qallunaag, or white man's winter school, in Yellowknife and had spent the summer looking for money jobs. It was at a Saturday night village social that the Inuit had discussed future plans with Jake. He had been attentive when they divulged their plans to buy a small boat. They would hunt seal. It is possible that they had expected some sound advice on this matter, but the fact was that Jake, a considerate listener, barely knew which was the bow and which was the stern in nautical matters, and as for hunting seal…

They proposed the buying of a small boat and equipping it with a large engine and it became obvious by the intensity of the sound being generated below the pier that they had acquired the large engine. The cousins reasoned that if the boat was small enough they could manhandle it across the ice. They would maneuver it in the same manner they would move a kayak. The large engine would allow them to crash through the pan ice, spring ice that was often too thick to break with a paddled kayak but too thin to walk on. They – Jake, Jerry and Pete – had discussed government grants, possible bank loans or credit at the Bay store. Jake's contribution to the discussion was an occasional nod of head or a 'I don't know about that', and here they were, a new boat and a God-awful racket machine fastened to it and the engine noise was now a muted roar. A vibrant deep mutter such as a trombone growl. That they had found the money was obvious.

With deceptive ease, they maneuvered the craft away from the beach. A cautious, slow advance was made towards the anchored fleet. A hesitant turn was accomplished and then more speed, resulting in a higher following wave. Jerry sat in the stern, the tiller in his right hand, left hand now busy with elated waving towards the pier and the smiling Jake, who waved both hands, did a formalized bow and raised his voice in a lusty, 'Go, man, go.'

The oversized engine, slung on the transom, had raised the bow high above the water and Pete was not helping the situation. He sat slightly back of amidships, his ass hanging over the starboard gunwale. They were now plowing a two-foot trough of water, and the sound of the exhaust was only a murmur, mixed with the noise of trucks, cranes and various pump engines. But, oh my, did it start to pop when Jerry wound the throttle up towards full open.

The boat was now beyond the pier with a full view of the work crews, the anchored ships and the crowd of friends and relatives who stood on the small hill above the beach offloading zone. One by one, the work crews stopped the machines and watched the white craft in what was now an insane water ballet.

The boys had spotted Janie and her sister Suzie, two of the local beauties who were amongst the cheering, waving crowd. These two would be in awe of the skilful handling of this quick marvelous little boat. The boys could almost hear the squeals of adulation.

Around it went, in tight white circles, with Pete and Jerry yelling and waving and Jake was caught up in the madness, and began jumping up and down and Jerry turned the throttle even farther and the bow lifted even higher and the blue sky could be seen under the curved hull. The engine crack, crack, cracked and a curled, white roost's tail of sparkling water piled up behind, then the engine noise was gone…

A squawking gull circled above the small, white boat now filling with water. The Arctic Ocean was rushing up the gunwales of the boat and Jerry was splashing his arms and Pete's mouth was wide open and both of them were looking at Jake across that sixty feet of infinity. Half the white boat was left, pointing at the blue sky, and both Pete and Jerry were splashing like little boys learning how to swim as the bow went underwater. Two black heads sat on top of the blue sea, framed by gray, lynx fur trim. The two mouths were open but there were no screams and two dark-blue parkas disappeared into the ice-blue depths, sinking down, bobbing up, down, up… Gone…

The chug, chug, chug of the fuel pump carried across the quiet of the Bay. A truck roared up the road with another load and Jake, hands thrust deep into parka pockets, stood on the pier, staring across the piercing cold water at the small oil slick, sixty feet from the cement and gravel-filled pier.

Chapter Sixteen

There are small powers, meager divinities and lesser gods who occasionally, in moods of frivolity, arrange circumstances in haphazard sequence, then, with a flagon of wine to hand, take positions of comfort that will afford the best viewing of that day's drama – how punitive man will cope with a new arrangement of the humdrum.

At six o'clock on a cold February morning, the raucous noise of the two-dollar alarm clock blasted the quiet of the bedroom. The blanket-covered lump moved and with grunts and snorts of protest, greeted the new morning. Michael 'Irish' Clow, recently promoted to lead radician and even more currently elevated to the lofty pinnacle of acting station chief, sat up and scratched. He had arrived at this temporary throne by reason of the permanent monarch abdicating briefly for reasons of rest and restoration of physical and mental well-being. For these ministrations the monarch had journeyed to the south, the land of sun and big boobs. Michael wished him a safe return for the temporary tenure of one week had been sufficient time to be wearied of the over-abundance of office routine and management protocol.

Being the boss was not a pleasant occupation. Stultifying as it was. The dining room was typical of the areas where Michael felt awkward. Representative of the change were the boisterous jests that had been the usual morning salutations but were now civilized 'Good mornings'.

Tony, the cook, had poured a cup of coffee for the station chief, a custom that was extended only to a station chief or the person who was the temporary station chief but it caused Michael some fluster. Tony stood, beside the table, waiting – a further annoyance.

'Some breakfast, Michael? Baste a couple of eggs?'

'I'll get some toast later. Thanks.'

'It's no trouble. I'll put some on for you. Rye bread?'

Dawson Pender, with coffee cup in hand, joined Michael for an informal management meet. In the process of staff reorganization Dawson was now the lead rad. A position he was very happy with: no shift work, no console watch and more of the folding green. It was a pleasant occupation and the thought had occurred that this would be a satisfying, permanent post.

'Morning, Dawson. We get anything new during the night?'

'All's quiet. The Canadian polar flight, number 871, was waiting eighteen minutes behind schedule, and was flying four hundred feet below her posted flight plan. No sweat. They acknowledged that our observations were correct.' Dawson continued, 'We're going to need another RF generator, like yesterday. The one that came back from test and calibration had two screws rattling around loose and then it went up in smoke.'

Michael frowned and said, 'I'll bet that caused some "God damn it to hell" yelling. Not your fault, but we are going to be long overdue with the monthly routines.'

'We have another week.'

'I'll call the main site and see what they can do. Anything else?'

'At six thirty, Jock slammed out of here without his morning tea. Said to tell you he would see you later.'

Jock was the Foxe Two 'H' mechanic responsible for light, water and sewage. He was answerable for hot water in the showers, repairs to leaky roofs, snow removal, and seventy-degree warmth in forty-below temperatures. A short, bristled Scotsman who was prone to excited reaction, he was an old-timer respected by the citizens at large.

Michael sipped some coffee and said, 'He's still in a knot about the Eskimo polishing the floors before washing them. I'll get Izaak outside. Out of sight, out of mind. Right?'

As though summoned by telepathy Izaak joined the meeting at the station chief's table where he proceeded to add a quarter cup of sugar to a three-quarters-full cup of coffee. Michael watched patiently and eventually the short, smiling man finished mixing the sugar and coffee. Conversation was further delayed whilst he applied brisk movements to finding tobacco and rolling a lumpy cigarette.

At last, exhaling large amounts of smoke in Michael's face, he said, 'Okay, boss, you okay today? Me, I'm going to be real busy.

Go-go all day for sure.'

'I hope so, Izaak. We need water yesterday.' Michael continued, 'Why didn't you get water on Friday? You told me you would. The main tank is dry and now we're on reserves. If you don't get some water up here PDQ, the shit will hit the fan and you, you'll be melting snow.'

'It's okay, boss. Friday I had to grease the D-8. She was squeaking bad, but all fixed and go like hell today.'

'Well, we have to have water today. No frigging around.'

'I'll chop damned hole quick and water be here by coffee time,' Izaak promised.

'It had better be today or you'll be shoveling snow into that snow-melting mother, and I tell you, that bugger makes for a long day.'

'Don't worry boss. I'll get water. We got no sweat, boss. We got lots of snow.'

Izaak's last remark was not exactly the truth. There is, in fact, very little snow in the Arctic. The Arctic is a desert with no precipitation and what snow there is comes on the wind and the wind piles the white stuff up against each and every obstruction but the bulk is carried to more distant lands. DEW-line sites were equipped with ice-melting equipment but ice had to be wrested from the four-foot-thick ocean covering, a tedious endeavor – in fact it was damned hard work.

A short time later, Michael heard the clank, clank, clank of the caterpillar and water tank – called an Athey Wagon – being piloted off the site. The white men were amazed by the quickness with which the Inuit acquired the manual skills to operate sophisticated heavy equipment. The 'Kabuna' were further astonished by the depth of understanding the native people quickly acquired concerning the inner workings of the internal combustion engine, gear boxes, pumps and all manner of mechanical devices that were newly arrived in this primitive land. Their aptitude was astonishing and an embarrassment for the 'Kabuna'. The white men attached great importance to formal training in technical fields but the Inuit, by the use of logic, native intelligence and astute observation, mastered demanding trades with ease. A large number of Inuit were employed to operate the large yellow and black road machinery and they did it with great skill.

Izaak had been hired three months earlier for general duties. Such duties included housekeeping of the common areas and the more demanding assignment of moving bulk goods such as garbage and site water. The garbage was transported four miles to a ravine, where, in the spring it would be covered with earth. During the winter the garbage accumulation became a mountainous treasure of frozen crud. Izaak much preferred hauling water.

In winter, the site's potable water was hauled three miles from a freshwater lake by means of a D-8 cat and trailer. The tracked trailer was fitted with a thousand-gallon tank and a small gasoline engine-driven pump. As the winter progressed the thickening ice dictated that Izaak chopped the water hole daily.

When the new hole had been drilled, Izaak would start the rackety air-cooled engine and watch the flak form of the hose swell with water. Assured that all was 'A-okay', he would retire to the leather seat of the big D-8 cat and there enjoy the satisfying engine roar and the magical puffs of the dense exhaust smoke.

In the station chief's office, Michael busied himself with the telephone, arranging a replacement for the toasted test equipment. That task was only just finished when the site 'H' mechanic made an entrance.

'Now then, Michael,' said Jock. 'What are we going to do about this situation?'

'Which situation are we at now, Jock?'

'We're out of water, lad, out of water, I say.'

'Not quite. We have the emergency supply and that's four hundred gallons. Right?'

'She'll be dry damned soon. Four hundred gallons is hardly a cup's worth. I tell you, Michael, if we go dry, it's I who will have those damned lines to bleed and I've better things to do than mess with that sorry job. So what about it, lad?'

'Izaak left for the lake twenty minutes ago.'

'Well then, I'd best be going down there. Speed things up a bit and give the lad a hand. Mind, there is a lot that needs my attention this morning.'

'Now, Jock, you're busy and Izaak will manage. It's his job.'

'I could get away for a few minutes. Save him some trouble with the pumping. We will be out of water here 'ere long lad.'

'What the hell. Okay, take a look but don't stay. You have other things to do.'

And minutes later a half-ton truck roared off across the tundra in hot pursuit of the tractor and water trailer.

Jock arrived as Izaak was maneuvering the water tank into position for backing out over the ice. Jock drove the truck up beside the large tracked machine and before the blue half-ton had fully stopped rolling, the door was flung open and the intrusive Scotchman was on the ice waving his arms.

Izaak left the glass-encased cab and clambered down four feet to enter into conversation with Jock. Ten minutes later the conference ended with Jock at the controls of the D-8 cat. There was some awkwardness as the machine lurched backwards over the ice and shortly the trailer skewed left. Jock stopped and corrected the trailer turning error by pulling ahead. Again a backwards lurching and a pull ahead to correct the problem, and after three such maneuvers, and some weaving to left and right, the tractor and water tank trailer combination was within five feet of the ice hole used by Izaak on previous visits. Two feet of ice had formed since the last pumping and the men busied themselves in the removal of the ice plug.

What exact sequence of events occurred then is not fully understood. The company inquiry determined that the D-8 cat had been parked in neutral with the Athey Wagon attached but by some supernatural means or telekinesis the Athey Wagon moved itself while still attached to the twelve-ton D-8 tracked vehicle. The supernatural movement of this heavy equipment resulted in the Athey Wagon becoming partially submerged up to half its length.

Izaak scrambled onto the cat and attempted to drive forwards, away from the black water, whilst Jock, half a second behind in comprehension, raced for the truck. The situation was balanced on a knife edge. The steel-ribbed cat tracks clawed and chewed at the ice and made a one-foot forwards advance away from the danger and shuddered to a stop. Izaak pulled the dual brake leavers full back and froze in that position. Jock yelled something as he wheeled the truck around and headed for the site.

At the dump, Nanook pawed at a mound of frozen cartons, coffee grounds and tin cans in angry frustration. The polar bear had been picking tidbits from the daily deposit for the past month and now a break in routine had brought no fresh garbage to the landfill site for the last four days. Nanook tossed his great white head back and forth, checking for the smell of food but, finding nothing, he headed across the narrow peninsula towards the distant pack ice. He could have gone the shorter route by retracing his earlier path but that was an emptiness he had already hunted.

Three miles across the peninsula, Izaak sat frozen to the brake levers, willing Jock's return but Jock was having trouble starting the snowplow-equipped road grader. The mammoth diesel-driven machine had the advantages of great weight and snow tires equipped with chains. The only machine for the extraction of a water wagon D-8 cat amalgamation in a difficult situation. At last, Jock triumphed over adversity, and with great enthusiasm, but little talent, headed back to the scene of the catastrophe.

At the morning coffee break Michael queried Dawson about the absent Izaak and Jock.

'Haven't seen either of them all morning, Michael.'

Michael explained his concern.

'They headed out for water after breakfast and they should have been back by now. I think I'll head down there. Want to come along for the ride?'

'Sure, give me ten minutes. I'll get my parka and meet you at the exit door.'

Before Michael had finished his coffee the snowplow went roaring past the dining room heading down the road to the water hole.

'Now what the hell?' Michael expostulated, when he realized what the unexpected engine noise was. He left in a rush, making a brief stop for Dawson, who was hurrying through the exit door, closing the zipper of his cold weather parka. When the truck crested the small hill between the site and the fresh water lake, Michael braked hard.

'Holy Christ!' was Michael's comment.

Dawson added the 'My God'.

The pristine snow-covered lake was punctured fifty feet from the shoreline and the D-8 sat like a yellow hornet, hauling at the half-submerged water tank. Izaak was still gripping the brake levers, a diminutive Hercules attempting the beaching of a strange beast from the deep, while Jock was maneuvering the massive road grader back along the twin tracks out on the ice. With no further waste of time Michael barreled the half-ton truck down to join them.

Nanook had maintained a steady lope across the tundra but at the crest of the peninsula he pulled up and cocked his head, confused by the strange sounds and smells that assaulted him. Up to that point his path had been a straight line to the sea and the shortest route was between the site buildings and the activity at the lake. To avoid a strange confrontation, he veered to the left, to the far end of the site. Nanook's pace slowed to a more investigative stroll and he was rewarded by the smell of food. A light, west wind carried traces of the cook's fried liver and bacon lunch preparations and Nanook's highly sensitized olfactory organ had detected the fragrance two miles away. His path was altered automatically.

At the lake, Michael, Dawson and Jock had managed a hook-up, using a heavy-duty tow chain between the front end of the D-8 and the tow bar of the snowplow. Without obvious strain, the snowplow slowly inched the D-8 with attached water wagon out and away from the jagged hole. In high jubilation, Izaak started yelling and everybody grinned and congratulated each other.

Izaak said something about, 'What I tell you, boss? See, I told you not to worry. No sweat.'

Michael shook his head and with a measure of sarcasm that escaped the Inuit said, 'Sure, but that's it. From now on, no shortcuts. You use the hose and pump.'

The men sorted out the chains and vehicles and headed back to work leaving Izaak with the job of filling the water tank.

Nanook padded up the center of the road along the length of the aluminum-sided building. Occasionally he paused and raised his head, casting about with his long snout, zeroing in on the tantalizing aroma. Rearing up on hind legs put his head level with the kitchen grill exhaust louver. Nanook planted himself in a boxer-like stance, left rear paw slightly forwards, claws turned slightly in. Foregoing a preliminary left jab, using an open-pawed right hook that would have done Ezzard Charles proud, Nanook opened up four feet of the kitchen wall.

Tony, the cook, was standing five feet to the side of the sudden change in his kitchen wall. He was chopping onions and for a moment was grateful for the breath of fresh air but when he realized that his tin sanctuary was being opened, and then noted the size of the can opener, he screamed.

Nanook was confused for in his past experience with cans that contained food, none had screamed. He backed up half a step and then with both paws he opened the wall even farther.

The large head coming through the wall of Tony's kitchen invoked a response that surprised everyone, especially Tony. Foolhardy courage stood revealed and with no further time wasted on hysterics, Tony grabbed the foam-filled fire extinguisher and attacked.

Nanook knew not what hit him. Grunting and snuffing, stopping only long enough to wipe with first one paw and then the other, the semi-blind bear made for the open tundra.

Michael and Dawson returning from the water tank launching were confronted by what appeared to be a rabid bear on the attack. Michael stood the truck on its nose but it was still a resounding encounter. The truck came to an abrupt stop and steam began boiling up from under the crumpled hood. When Michael and Dawson exited the broken vehicle, the bear was wrapped around the front of the truck with a broken neck.

A month later, at the Saturday night bar, the tanned and mounted bearskin rug was presented to the site hero, Tony 'Quick Draw' Delorme, fryer of onions and bear destroyer extraordinaire.

Chapter Seventeen

At the Foxe Main lower camp, squatting four hundred feet from the transient dormitories, was the long steel Quonset hut used as a dining hall. A rectangular, plywood shelter had been added to the half-circle-shaped end of the structure to provide a buffer zone between the frigid Arctic and the cafeteria. The floor of the plywood entryway was always a sheet of ice and mud and during the dining hours, the walls were thickly hung with grease and mud-splotched air force-issue Arctic parkas.

Four lines of tables paraded one hundred feet to the stainless steel serving counter. Equally spaced along the length of the tabletops, clusters of ketchup bottles, serviette dispensers and salt and peppers interrupted the uniform neatness. Crammed in under the length of the tables, backless wooden benches crowded into the aisles. Tables, benches, dispensers, were arranged with military precision.

Separating the dining room and the kitchen, a three-foot-high serving counter supported stacks of porcelain plates, soup bowls, trays of knives and forks and two rows of empty stainless steel warming pans. Behind the counter was the institutional kitchen machinery – the shiny black fry grills, walk-in freezers, square, solid chopping tables were arranged for efficiency. Neon light reflected brightly off the hanging multitude of whisks, soup ladles, egg pans and specialty pans. Everything in its place and a place for everything.

In the center of the kitchen area, a lank-haired man was sitting on a three-foot-high stool drinking from a white mug. On the table at his elbow the whisky bottle was down to the last inch of amber. Behind him a large commercial floor-model food mixer grumbled and whined. In the large stainless steel bowl, a white glob, burbled protest at the constantly revolving paddles that folded and curled the viscous-textured dough.

Lester Karpas was the Foxe Main baker and this was his first shift after a weekend break. His shift had begun at 2200 hours and the work included the baking of eighty loaves of bread, twenty cakes, twelve pies and in his spare time, maybe whip up some sugar-coated donuts.

The overhead neon was harsh with Lester. It revealed the thinning hair hanging out below the chef-style white cap, an unshaven face and worse, it shone on the wet lines below the dark-blue eyes.

At 1400 hours, eight hours before his shift, Lester had tried phoning home. He had made repeated attempts on Friday night, Saturday and again Sunday, to speak with Annette, his wife for five years. She was gone. Not out for the evening. Gone. Moved. No one knew where. Lester had spoken with the building manager who had told him, 'She's gone. I don't know where. She turned in the key last Monday.'

Lester had been south for three weeks in September. The first week had been great, for Annette's mother had taken the kids, and Lester and Annette had orgied. Indulged to excess, slept late, partied late and sated their six-month appetites.

On Sunday, Mum had brought the kids back and it was time for serious things. Serious things like the Karpas family's board meeting. It was a game they had played, even before their marriage. A talk and plan session. In the years when the marriage was a new adventure, there had been bills and children and dreams and 'the plan'. They would buy a bakery, a small neighborhood place, a specialty shop where Annette would be in charge of the front counter with a part-time girl on Fridays and Saturdays. Lester would bake. One part-time helper, maybe two. Fresh bread daily. A few pastries, wedding cakes, birthday cakes but mostly wedding cakes. Big money in wedding cakes and the decorating. Annette would do the decorating.

Lester and Annette would talk for long hours. In the early morning, before daybreak, they would still be planning, revising the budget, discussing their future. How much here, how much there. During the first years of the marriage, the budget had been a simple matter. So much in, deduct monies spent and the remainder was savings. You didn't have to be an Einstein. They had arrived at expenses by averaging the costs of the first married years. Rent, food and personal needs. All in black and white.

The big money opportunity changed things. A shortcut to their pot of gold. They had talked all night. In two years, three at the most, they could make and save ten thousand if Lester took a job with Federal Electric. Something called the DEW-line. It would be tough. Lester in isolation and Annette with two babies. But after that they would be on easy street. Their own business and debt free.

Two months before Lester's R and R, Annette had found the store that they wanted. She had read the 'for sale' ad and talked to the owner, Lars Anderson, who was sixty and making plans for a sun-filled retirement in Arizona. Ten thousand would cover the lease and equipment and now after a week of rest it was time for the Karpas family's board meeting. The get-rich-quick scheme had worked. The proof was the bank book balance of nine thousand, one hundred and eighty-four dollars.

'It was the dentist. Jerry needed so much work and he was so brave, but it took five visits, and then the rent went up... otherwise there would be ten thousand.'

'Hell, honey, it's okay. Look, nine thousand. We're rich, or damned near, so I'll go talk to the guy.'

On Monday, with the bank book for proof of the nine thousand, Lester had met with Lars Anderson. Lester and Lars enjoyed a coffee and Lester explained the need for a six-month delay. Not a long time, and then spring. Spring, the time of new life. But this was now and Lars could foresee six months of snow and remembered well how cold January can be.

'How about a mortgage? I could carry you. This place would pay, believe me.'

'I couldn't do that, Lars. We, Annette and I, neither of us have had much to do with business, financing, that kind of thing. What we do know is that we had better start debt free. I'm a baker, and the idea of owing money and being told how to run things... You know? I couldn't do it. Look, in six months, I'll have the ten and another two or three thousand to run the business with. I make big money in the north. Give me three months. Twelve weeks.'

Lars said nothing. He sat looking at the large, black ovens, thinking. In twelve weeks, the snow would be two feet deep in the parking lot and in twelve weeks new friends, and neighbors could be gathering at an Arizona barbecue.

'Lester, I would like to help you. You're a fine young man, a good baker, but this arthritis of mine is really something in the winter. It gets so bad I can't move this right arm. If you get the ten thousand together by the thirty-first, I'll be here. Otherwise... I'm sorry. I've been holding for a month because you made the first offer but there is another guy and he is ready now.'

There had been a long silence and finally Lester had set down his coffee cup and said, 'I'll talk to Annette, but I can't promise much. We were sure there would be enough, but things came up. The dentist... What the hell, I'll try. I'll let you know.'

The sound of the mixer laboring with the thickening dough brought Lester back to the 2:00 A.M. Arctic bakery. He emptied what was left of the whisky into his cup before pushing the red stop button on the straining paddles. He stared a long time into the wave-shaped dough, and then, head tilted back, he drained the cup.

Annette had cried. A long deep cry. Lester had reasoned with her and explained that they would find another bakery. In the meantime, he would go back north and she could look and when she found another bakery, they would pay cash. No delays next time. She had sat crying, not really listening, and finally he had gone to bed. Lester had awakened at 4:00 A.M. and found her writing a list.

'A list of clothes for me and the kids: dresses, shoes, winter coats, and while I'm at it, a new fridge. That old thing there grows mould and keeps me awake.'

'Take it easy, honey. Sure, you're right. We get the kids new clothes, you too, but look, if we save now, in six months we'll have fifteen thousand and you know what that will mean? Financial independence.'

'I know what it means to me, Lester old buddy. I'll be talking like a six-year-old. I'll be the laughing stock of the neighborhood because I never go anywhere. Christ, my mother had a better time when my father went to war. At least there were other women in the same boat. Well, if I'm going to stare at these walls for six months I want pictures on them. So if you want fifteen thousand, you had better start thinking about another year.'

'Aw, honey. Look, take a thousand. As soon as the stores open we'll go shopping. I'll come with you. A new coat and new dresses. We'll get something really classy. Okay? Let's go to bed and first thing in the morning it's away downtown.'

Annette had looked like a fashion model, the best-dressed woman amongst the dozens who were gathered in the concrete and marble airport departure rotunda. Lester paid little attention to the crowd, well maybe a quick glance at the odd redhead, but Annette, Annette had been radiant. Her black hair softly framing the delightful brown eyes, her exquisite mouth, and dainty nose. Every inch of her five feet was perfection, at least they were to Lester. She had driven Lester to the airport. They had dropped the kids at Mum's and Annette had proved to Lester that she would have no trouble driving the new Mustang in the city. She was a good driver.

'So really, darling. Don't worry. I'll be all right.'

And Lester had had to agree.

They had made a new 'plan'. Annette would check out two possibilities that they had found in the 'businesses for sale' column in the evening paper and she would further solicit several of the real estate offices for possibilities. If these efforts failed, they were prepared to open a bakery in a new shopping center and build the trade from the ground upwards. Lester was resigned to another year of isolation but with another year of DEW-line money their problems would be over. Lester tightened his seatbelt and smiled through the porthole window at the great-looking doll who was waving goodbye.

And now she had gone, address unknown. Lester switched on a light in the small storeroom at the back of the kitchen and after some rummaging around, he produced, with a sardonic grin, a bottle of Hennessy Three Star Brandy. The remains of the Christmas plum pudding.

Back in the neon-lit kitchen, he filled the white coffee mug three-quarters full, had a short drink, and then back to work. He spread a coating of flour across the top of the large table by the mixing bowl, and again he stopped, staring at the patterns his hand had made in the flour.

Friday, last Friday, had been mail day and the expected monthly bank statement had been saved for last. He had held it back intentionally, waiting to savor the size of the new balance. Annette's weekly letter had been the usual two-page list of generalities. Terrible weather, some small problem with the car and the kids were recovering from a virus, all my love, Annette. The children's letters were delightful. One page from each, done with crayons, in large awkward letters telling him to hurry home.

His final envelope – white, with window – was opened with drawn-out precision, building the once-a-month enjoyment that he experienced with reading the forward balance, and then down the right-hand column to current balance. But the one on Friday was a joke, a stupid mistake made by idiots. There were morons messing around with his money. Eight dollars and forty cents was the last figure on the page and it was an overdraft! This couldn't be his account. Christ, he had over ten, well almost ten thousand dollars in that lousy bank. What the hell was the matter with them?

It had taken two hours of pleadings and promising God knows what and he had finally arranged for a phone line south and he had caught the bank manager on his way out of the office.

The man's voice had been impersonal and officious.

'Yes, the account is a bit in arrears, but we will delay the processing of the service charges incurred. We value your business. There will be the usual deposit on the fifteenth? Good. Very good. I see no problem. You're a valued customer, Mr. Karpas, and this incident is no doubt an oversight by Mrs. Karpas. Certainly. By the way, how is the weather up there?'

Lester felt like he had been smashed on the head with a fence post. He reeled back to his room and sat for over an hour rocking back and forth on the edge of the camp bed.

Staring at the white frosted window with vacant eyes. He roused himself at last and fumbled a bottle from the bottom drawer of the nearby dresser and tipping his head back he had taken one long drink after another.

Friday and Saturday nights were his scheduled time off. He drank and stayed drunk until Sunday morning when he had realized that he had yet to talk with Annette. MacGonigle was with him and he had been Lester's confidant since sometime Saturday. Mac had talked to Lester, arguing that he should sleep and phone Annette when he woke up. There would be a good reason. Maybe she had found a bakery and it was a cash deal. Call her in the morning, but Lester wouldn't wait and he started bothering people at 5:00 A.M.

He tried the home number for three hours, much to the annoyance of the Quebec City long-distance operators. No one answered. He phoned Annette's mother but she hadn't seen her all week. The kids were there.

'No, I don't mind, Lester. After all, they are my grandchildren. It's no problem.'

Nothing was a problem to anyone. At last he got through to the apartment manager.

'Mrs. Karpas? She left. Last Monday. Cleaned it right out. How the hell would I know? Look, I'm sorry, but I don't know. If I hear anything…'

Lester stumbled back to his room and after a short sleep and a shower, dragged himself to work.

The silence of the shiny kitchen was occasionally interrupted by a freezer motor starting up but the low-level hum did nothing to alleviate the tomb-like hush. The dough in the mixing bowl stiffened, and became unmanageable. The plop of water from the leaky hot water tap was a startling clear ping, loud against the occasional penetration of the wind's low moaning.

Knotted to an overhead support structure above the neon lights, a twisted apron hung straight down, supporting the slowly turning lank-haired body. Mouth gaping, dark-blue eyes wide open, unshaven, pale face with dried-up tear stains on the cheeks.

On Tuesday morning, when the large doors at the end of the dining hall started banging open, and men hurried the shedding of gloves and parkas, pushing and shoving for position in the queue at the steaming trays of food, a few – six guys at most – stopped and read a new sign pinned up in the drab entry hall.

'NO HANGING AROUND IN THE KITCHEN.'

Chapter Eighteen

On Saturday morning the sun burned through the gray of winter and the sky was left sparkling blue and fluffy white, an abandonment of the mundane that would have made Monet proud with scattered reds, yellows and greens across the usual brown texture that was the tundra.

It was Jake's day off; a day for swamping out the crud from under the bed, or for parking his ass on a chair in the sun with his feet up, contemplating his navel day. A 'no shave, no shower' day or a 'watch the laundry stuff revolve past the washing machine window' day. A day for a change in the eat, work and sleep routine. What the hell, there's more to life than clean socks. Jake elected for a walk to town. To the Hudson Bay store, a two-mile stroll along the beach.

Above the hundreds of snow-melt lakes and ponds, the birds of summer wheeled and dove, shredding the summer wind song with raucous squawks and shrieks. On a distant ridge, three children, free of winter parkas, romped, adding laughter and children's clamor to the birds' shrill calls.

The Hudson Bay store manager, Jack Cookson, greeted Jake warmly on his entrance into the Cambridge Bay commercial center. The Inuit women, who were in attendance, politely covered their welcome smiles and tee-hees with a palm of their hand. Jake imitated their good manners by covering his mouth with an open palm and all the Inuit laughed.

Jake strode directly to the back counter, the candy counter with the glass jars of green and red jujubes and jelly beans and black and red licorice sticks and seven varieties of suckers. He waved dramatically, beckoning with both hands to the assembly of Inuit and a dozen round-eyed children ran to Jake. He pointed at the candy jars and the children nodded and the clerk behind the counter spilled a quarter-pound of red, black and green jelly beans into a small paper bag which Jake presented to the first child. In turn, each of the small black heads at Jake's knees made a selection and each was presented with the gift and responded with a very solemn, 'Thank you, Jake,' and a lovely shy smile.

When the ceremony was completed, Jake joined Jack Cookson and the Cambridge Bay resident Mountie corporal, Donald Tighe, who had wandered in, and the three stood with smiles and small talk, enjoying the pleasure of a Saturday afternoon conversation.

'So, Jake, a day off? No Russian rockets to worry about?'

Jake grinned at the Mountie and said, 'Two days, and I have it on good authority that the Russians take Saturdays off, so why shouldn't I? How have you been, Corporal?'

'Any better and I'd be a runaway.'

Jake said, 'You've been away for awhile? Out screwing around with that Jeannette McDonald? Right.'

'No, I leave that movie stuff for Nelson Eddy. What I do is spring routines; the headcount, how many born, how many died. Spring procedures. Checking that the constituents aren't smuggling any Russian vodka across the ice on dark nights.'

The store manager asked Jake about sea-lift but Jake had nothing definite.

'In the fall – September, October. No word yet.'

Jake asked the Mountie about the fishing.

'Is there anywhere close? I've heard that I might get some char out of the river. Is that right, Corporal?'

The corporal was a large man. Three inches taller than Jake. His hair was gray and he had dark-blue eyes above a pug nose, a firm mouth and square chin. A square block of a man.

'Call me Don. That corporal stuff makes me sound like some kind of military. Yes, there are fish in the river and if I had the time, I'd be out with a spinning rod and a Red Devil with a three-gang hook. By the way, I was thinking about you this morning.' He smiled at Jake and continued, 'Yes, I was thinking you are just about the right guy.'

'What's this? A wanted poster on me has shown up?'

'Nothing like that. No, what I was remembering was your broad back.' The Mountie continued, 'It happens that I'm in need of some help.'

'A small task for a broad back?'

'Something like that. I need a volunteer and I think I could find a spot of rum to offer as a gratuity.'

'Well now, I think you may have recruited a volunteer. What do you need?'

'It's our outboard motor. We have it on a rack, six feet in the air and twenty feet from the water and that is too high and too far for me to move alone.' The corporal continued, 'Gauche and Rogers won't be back from the eastern patrol for a week so here I am. Looking for help. How about it?'

'No problem, Don. Give me a minute and I'll be with you. I need some cigarettes and razor blades. I can't get those Wilkinson Swords at the site. Say, I'm walking. When we finish, will you give me a ride back?'

'No sweat, Jake. I'll get you home.'

For the first mile, beyond the village, the road wandered carelessly across the tundra, eventually arriving at the rock-studded Cambridge River. Here, there was a Bailey bridge crossing, and then the road curved up a small hill. At the top of the hill, the road narrowed to a thin path that crept past a white picket fence. It is there that the village buried their dead. The fence isolated a multitude of small, white crosses from the surrounding desolation.

There was a dramatic contrast between the uniform neatness of the graveyard and the surrounding disarray of black granite and brown tundra. Jake asked the Mountie to stop. The men rolled the truck windows down and with the truck quiet, bird calls, and the soft sounds of summer breezes drifted about them.

They sat a minute and then, without a word spoken, both left the truck and entered the neat graveyard. The small – none larger than four feet long – mounds were aligned with the methodical exactness of checkerboard squares, each small mound guarded by a very erect two-foot-high white cross. Jake spent several minutes reading names and dates and then turned to the Mountie.

'Jeez! They were all kids.'

'Right you are, Jake. Children for the most part. It happens in the spring, the burying that is. When the ice goes out and the land thaws they can dig in the tundra, clear some rocks and bury the children. The black-robed priest followed by the Eskimos. Very solemn it is. It's not that long ago that there were no crosses, no trees, no crosses, but now the church has a fund. A burial fund and each child goes with a cross. A small cross but that is a splendid thing in this place of no trees.'

With no further talk the men returned to the truck and drove on. With Jake's help the small job of engine moving was accomplished and in a very short time the two convened in the kitchen. Don poured a full measure of rum and the two sat, at ease, a pleasant end to a grunt and groan task.

'I owe you, Jake. That sucker was even heavier than I remembered. Thank you.'

'No sweat. I needed the outing.'

'So, Jake, where do you call home? You sound like a down-easterner.'

'Well, you got that right. A farm ten miles west of Fredericton.'

'Do some fishing out there, Jake?'

'A bit, in the St. John and Nackawic rivers. They were good at one time but there was no money fishing so I joined up.'

'Navy?'

'Ya. I did one tour on the *Bonny*, the aircraft carrier.'

'Aye. I know of her and you were on her?'

'Uh-huh, two years of destroyers and then the grand lady.'

'That boat out there on the beach is a bit smaller than you're used to.'

'For sure, it is, but, Donald, you haven't told me. How is the fishing, now that the ice is out?'

'Right. You're a fisherman.'

'Not to blow my own horn, Donald, but it is said that I'm the Izaak Walton of the St. John River. Why, I was using a split bamboo before I could ride a bicycle. Well maybe I'm exaggerating.'

'It's that time of year, Jake, when the char will be feeding now that the ice has been blown out of the bay. It would be a fine time out there with a soft westerly and fish lining up to jump into the boat.'

'When do you want to go? I'll get my rod and I've got some down-home lures that are almost a guarantee.'

'I can't get away for two weeks, Jake, what with Gauche and Rogers on patrol. But what about you? Maybe someone at the site, somebody else with you. You can't be out there alone. It's not safe.'

'Okay, I have two buddies who are suffering some cabin fever, hot damn. This will be great. You're sure? What time? Early, if you don't mind.'

'Not too early, Jake. Make it around eight. I need my Sunday morning beauty sleep.'

'This is terrific but how about licenses? Say, I'd better get back and line things up. Two guys be all right?'

'We can arrange the licenses tomorrow when we know who will be with you. Finish your drink and I'll run you back to the site.'

Gord and Tully listened to Jake's announcement with a mixture of incredulous disbelief and the joyous exuberance that would have been expected with the winning of a sweepstake.

'No shit. They'll lend us the boat? Jeez, I haven't been out of this stinking hole for three months. I've got to find my fishing pole and my hat. Got to have my hat.'

This soliloquy from Tully, a medium-sized, red-haired, green-eyed Newfie. Tully was the Cam Main North of Seventy Shit Sifters court jester. An impish grin was his trademark and his humor, rough in presentation, invariably involved a Newfie fisherman.

He roared off, still muttering, leaving Jake and Gordon Katler to finalize the more pertinent details. Gordon was overweight, stocky and rotund depending upon who described him. He never hurried and every action was deliberate from the positioning of his hands at rest in his lap to the exact parting of his thinning hair. Laugh lines etched wrinkles in the round face. A quiet, pleasant person.

'So, Jake. It promises to be a splendid day. We can catch an early breakfast, have the truck loaded, and be away by seven fifteen. I'll check around for a truck and make sure of the gas. What about gas for the outboard? We'll need white gas for it.'

Jake nodded and said, 'White gas for sure, but we'd better use theirs. We don't know what kind of a mixture they burn.'

Gordon said, 'We should go up to the Hudson Bay store. Buy a jar of salmon eggs and some new line and I need a couple of hooks. What about licenses?'

Jake leaned back, adjusting his bulk in the modified to extra-large armchair and said, 'Slow and easy, Gord. We get the licenses from the corporal in the morning but we will need lunches. Maybe Tully can take care of that. You arrange for the truck and I'll see the station chief about leaving the site. You know the rules about being off the base.'

'Oh sure. Have to get permission. Declare the purpose bullshit, but that's to keep track of people in foul weather.'

'It's the rule, Gordon. It's a good idea and it's no sweat and the boss will be glad to see some fresh fish. We can turn the catch over to the kitchen when we get back.'

'What about refreshment, Jake? Emergency de-icer.'

'We'll be careful there with it being Mountie's boat and all. We don't need an arrest ticket for drunk driving or illegal possession, but maybe a bottle for medicinal purposes.'

'Okay. I'll find a truck and see you later.'

The Sunday morning breakfast was a short pause between checking supplies and loading the truck. The day was everything God had promised Adam, a soft west wind had washed the sky blue and left the bay waters ice free. The road from the site to town was a straight path to the harbor. At the site boundary, white flagpoles flanked the wide, gravel track and on this morning, Canadian and American flags flapped proudly at the top of the fifty-foot white poles.

Half a mile beyond the flags, the road forked, the left fork ending a mile farther along at the airport terminal. The right track carried on in a gentle curve above the beach for two miles, where it entered the settlement, passing in front of the hospital. The road through town was empty and the red, blue and green-roofed houses were quiet. Two small Inuit boys poked around in the waters lapping on the beach below the Bay store, and, except for them, nothing else stirred.

Tully broke the silence.

'You'd think there would be someone around. Out, enjoying the sunshine.'

Jake explained.

'There was a big party at the DOT last night for a couple of guys going south and I bet they tied on a good one.'

Douglas met them with an offer of coffee, licenses were issued and formalities of which next-of-kin was to be notified were completed. There were cans of white gas and lifejackets at the boat launch.

Douglas said of the lifejackets, 'They'll be as much use as a snowball in hell if you need them in that water.'

The Mountie checked that the oars were on board and loose gear was stored and that the men had brought cold-weather clothing. In his words, 'You never know where you might find an iceberg.'

With no further commotion, the sailors put to sea.

Tully muttered, 'Me Mither was like that. Fussing, always fussing.'

The small boat put-put-putted across the bay and into the broad reach of Victoria Strait, heading east by northeast. There they met a light chop and freshening breeze but the day remained balmy. The men lounged on the thwarts, soaking up the sunshine.

The silence was broken by Gordon who asked, 'I wonder if Franklin had any sunny days when he was here?'

Tully's response was, 'Franklin who?'

It was a minute before Gordon spoke.

'You are fortunate that today you have in your company an authoritative voice on the legendary Sir John Franklin. It will be my pleasure to fill another gap in your pedestrian education. Concerning that icon in Canadian history, Franklin, I know a great deal about him because some generations back he was a great-great uncle. Yes a direct blood tie due to my English grandparents. He was my boyhood hero and I am still a great admirer of the man.

'He was born in 1786 and died in 1847, right out there,' and Gordon waved his hand towards the eastern horizon. 'He was Royal Navy. Fought at the battle of Trafalgar and then in the early 1800s explored the western Arctic. He did some mapping of the Coppermine River and the Mackenzie and then spent time charting the western Arctic coastline. In 1845, in command of two vessels, the *Erebus* and the *Terror*, he set out to find the North West Passage, a northern route to China. He wintered on Baffin Island and in the spring of 1847 headed south but, in Victoria Strait, their way was blocked by thick pack ice. Gentlemen, this is Victoria Strait. Franklin died in this area on June 11, 1847. Three hundred and five survivors headed south, looking for a Hudson Bay post but one and all died of starvation and scurvy.

'For the next ten years the Royal Navy searched for answers and they finally found a record of the journey in a cairn of rocks about a hundred miles south of here, but they never found Franklin. It was because of the number of search parties looking for Franklin that the Arctic became British and thus Canadian.'

Jake said, 'Gordon, that is amazing and all that Canadian history happened here. I had no idea. Can you imagine spending a winter up here on a wooden boat? Hearts of oak and all the stuff. It would have been bloody hell. You're right on about John Franklin. He was some kind of sailor and you say his grave wasn't found?'

'Not a trace.'

The men sat fishing quietly, and eventually a small sculpin was caught and the sun began its descent through the afternoon sky. A lengthening white trace in the all-blue sky was the first distraction in two hours. The contrail of the Vancouver-bound polar flight proved that there was other life left on earth. The flat sea and fresh air were hypnotic and the gentle rocking of the boat had reduced the three fishermen to a semiconscious state and now magic was performed in the heavens as the blue sky was split from east to west by the widening wedge of the aircraft's vapor trail.

Jake stretched and scratched and then with a solemn voice said, 'The sky god has drawn a line through his front yard. I wonder if he is annoyed with us?'

Tully looked at him for a moment before asking, 'You having a headache? Any cramps or disorders?'

Jake gave him a grin and said, 'Fifty years ago, that contrail up there would have looked as strange to the Eskimos as a couple of Martians would look to us.'

After the polar flight, the men settled back, returning to the earlier lethargy and the afternoon drifted by. Gradually the blue western sky behind the men disintegrated and storm clouds began piling up above the horizon and the flat water of the bay began building small white caps.

The sun, the orange and white DOT radio tower and the multicolored houses of the distant village were obscured in a white mist. Without a word, Tully, who had been dozing in the stern, cranked up the outboard and headed in. He was too late. A warm-weather fog engulfed them and Tully slowed the outboard speed to dead slow. So much for Sunday afternoon.

Jake spoke first.

'This must be one of those Arctic fogs we heard 'bout in Streator.

You remember. They called it a convection or something.'

'It's called advection,' Gordon corrected. 'But I understood they were a winter phenomenon caused by cold air blowing across warm water.'

Tully spoke up to say, 'Well, the water ain't warm.'

'Relatively warm,' Gordon qualified his argument. 'There must be a cold air mass coming in.'

'Does that mean we're going to get some wind?' Jake asked.

Gordon confirmed, 'You can bet on it.'

'We'll be okay if we head straight for shore. Right? So keep the speed down, Tully, hold a westerly direction and we'll be on the beach in ten minutes and back at camp for dinner.'

Jake's positive attitude was reassuring. Slowly they poked their way through the cold cloud of condensed vapor. The fog engulfed them, shut them off from all points of reference and ineffectively they brushed with their hands at the thickening whiteness.

Tully, in the stern, said, 'There's nothing out there. It's like that mystery trip, a hundred-dollar vacation, I heard about. A guy from Newfoundland was looking for an adventure, something unusual, away from the crowd, so to speak.'

Jake interrupted the story with, 'We're there, Tully, I just saw some shoreline straight ahead.'

Some dilution of the white veil allowed the men an opaque glimpse of a blue-green iceberg rising from the gray-green water. Tully slowed the boat's forward movement and Jake, with surprising agility, hopped over the bow. With the bowline in his hand, he scrambled away and soon his muffled voice was heard in the fog.

'Okay. I've got it tied up.'

Gordon and Tully checked for loose gear and then joined him.

Jake greeted them with, 'I don't recall any icebergs this big anywhere in Cambridge Bay. How about it, Gordon? Does this real estate ring any bells?'

'There hasn't been any ice on the radar screen for a month, more like two months. Am I right, Tully?'

'There is nothing like this in my worst dreams so where in hell have we got to?'

Jake offered a weak platitude.

'We were heading towards the beach so we won't be that far from the site, and we'll know for sure, as fast as the fog lifts and we can see the DOT tower.' He continued, 'So what do you say, how about some lunch, a sip of the nectar and, Tully, I want to hear that story about the Newfie on the hundred-dollar "Mystery Holiday Adventure Trip".'

The boys settled down, preparing themselves for an uncertain stay and Tully launched into the story.

'Seems a guy looking for a cheap holiday tells the agent behind the counter that he wants the hundred-dollar adventure trip. The one advertised in the window.'

Gordon interrupted, 'Sounds like a Saturday night train ride to Sudbury.'

Tully shook his head and said, 'No, not Sudbury. The agent takes the Newfie's money, hands him a ticket and hits him over the head with a blackjack. He then drags the unconscious boyo into the back room.'

Jake grinned and said, 'Definitely sounds like a five-star Halifax cocktail lounge.'

Tulley continued.

'About fifteen minutes later a French Canadian wanders in and requests a ticket, the one-hundred-dollar adventure trip. Again the agent takes the money, gives the man a ticket, hits him over the head and drags him into the back room. Several hours later the holiday kids wake up in a row boat somewhere in the middle of an ocean. The French Canadian says to his companion, "Gee, I wonder if they serve drinks on this lousy trip?" "They didn't last year," replies the Newfie.

Jake and Douglas roared with laughter.

The men looked for soft spots amongst the hard as granite ice ridges and eventually settled down, preparing themselves for an unpleasant wait. The wind awoke them. A steady forty-knot, bone-chilling east wind, and the noise, an alarming, teeth-grinding dissonance that caused immediate anxiety about the boat. The stout craft was as they had left it, tied with the painter to a large wooden post that protruded from the ice much like an elephant's tusk.

The Cambridge Bay transport vehicle had stopped moving and the fog had gone, replaced by rainy day visibility and the blue waters of the bay were now a grinding, rasping, layer of broken ice. Large, irregular-shaped white pancakes of ice being moved by the wind. The ice pack was back and now filled the bay, an agitated mass that rose and fell with wavelike movement. Each piece was playing 'crowd your neighbor', edge riding up on neighboring edge, forming new patterns in the black sea water and the ragged moving kaleidoscope stretched away to the dim horizon.

Jake, Tully and Gordon scrambled out of the protective pocket and clambered the ten-foot elevation that was the pinnacle of their domain. No one spoke; each reconnoitering their position. Shortly the three squatted down, crowding together, face to face and out of the wind.

Jake opened the conference.

'This chunk of ice has moved right along. It has blown out into the bay. It's been a grand midnight sail but now we're surrounded by ice and we won't be leaving till we get some blue water.

Gordon asked, 'How long do you figure, Jake?'

Jake thought a moment.

'Tomorrow or maybe early morning of the next day. You know the winds as well as I.'

The men returned to the boat and took an inventory. There wasn't much: seven sandwiches, three cans of juice, twenty-odd ounces of whisky, thirty cigarettes and twenty-one matches.

Tully jumped up in excitement.

'We've got gas. There's still a full tank of gas.'

'Good thinking, Tully,' said Jake. 'At least we won't freeze. Right, Gordon?'

'Right, Jake. We can keep a slow fire going and there is a lot of wood in that tree we're tied up to.'

Tully had a question.

'What kind of tree grows in ice and since when do any trees grow in the Arctic?'

No one had an answer.

The men returned to the boat for another look at the moored craft. The timber to which the boat was tied was indeed stout.

Marks of hand-hewn axe cuts were evident and Jake declared, 'There is only one tool that leaves marks like that. A draw plane. A two-handed blade that was pulled through wood to shape or flatten. A tool used by shipwrights a hundred years ago. In any case we have firewood. Let's get down out of this wind while we wait.'

It was a long wait. A sleep and wake and stare at nothing wait and more sleep.

Gordon the optimist said, 'Come morning, things will be all right.'

Tully was skeptical and loudly voiced his opinion.

'All right? All right, you say? You're daft if you think this will ever be all right.'

Jake tried for some humor, something about a chicken ranch but he was ignored and the men pulled and twisted the parkas up and over their heads. Jake joined them in the imitation ostrich act and the casual observer could have mistaken them for walruses, resting after a hard day.

At four thirty there was movement amongst the huddled cocoons and the largest of the three blobs emerged to check his watch. He was smiling when he roused his buddies.

'We've got a west wind.'

Gordon's head appeared and he said, 'That's great. We could be home for breakfast.'

Tully manipulated the situation with, 'There's no need to starve ourselves. A small tot and sunrise will be upon us.'

Several hours after sunrise, under the cloud-free blue sky, the sparkling waters rippled lightly under the gentle west wind. The bay was practically ice free when a small skin-covered kayak, deftly paddled by a very small Inuit, silently approached the occupied iceberg. Curious about the beached boat he paddled closer and what he saw next so astonished him that he lost the rhythm of his paddling. Three 'Kabuna' appeared, three large, slovenly, red-eyed, crazy white men. The eight-year-old sat perplexed. In due time he recognized his friend.

'You sleep here, Jake?'

'Yes. You could say that.'

'That's a very hard sleeping bench, Jake.'

Without further conversation he paddled off and the men quickly followed in their craft. There was a final look at their overnight accommodation before they steered to the Mountie's dock and

Gordon asked, 'I wonder if our mooring post was an oak that came from England a hundred years ago?'

Jake said, 'That's as good an explanation as any for trees that grow out of icebergs. But if it did come from England, I have to say that you have some powerhouse of a guardian uncle watching over you.'

Chapter Nineteen

During the month of March, George spent a lot of time resting in the sun. He had built a tanning salon. It was a substantial wooden box, made from three-quarter-inch plywood and was eight feet long and four feet wide. The top was four feet high and the walls were tapered, to a two-foot, six-inch-high end panel. The top, a single sheet of three-quarter-inch plywood, had been milled, and now formed a hinged doorframe with openings left for panels. The openings were covered with two sheets of clear plastic. The air gap between the clear plastic was insulation against the minus-thirty-degree outside temperature.

The other side of the coin was, if George fell asleep and a chance cloud blocked the sun's rays, for even so brief a time as five minutes, George's naked flesh would turn blue. And that was why, beside the executive phone, the beer cooler and the stack of *Playboy* back issues, there lay an emergency, ready to use, down-filled sleeping bag. George could be in the bag, with only his large nose protruding, in fifty seconds and he had accomplished this survival routine on two occasions in the past week.

George stretched, yawned and scratched and patted a damp brow dry with a fluffy white towel. Another stretch accompanied with a loud yawn, and George made use of the black telephone. There was a short time before George spoke.

'Martin? George here. Will you be at the game? Same place, Warehouse Number Two. Great. There will be seven of us. Okay. See you.'

Once again George dialed and spoke.

'George Donner here. May I speak with Doc? It is? Good. I am calling in regards to the Saturday night game. Right. Several people have mentioned your name and it would be my pleasure if you were able to attend.' George listened and then said, 'Right. At Pin Main. You can catch a lateral flight tomorrow morning. Saturday. Right, and there is a return flight Sunday at 1600 hours. There won't be a problem. Mention my name to Bill Classen, the traffic controller over there. Sure, he's at the hangar.' Again George listened and then said, 'Good, see you tomorrow night.'

George Donner was the Pin sector supply specialist, the man in charge of all goods. The procurement, distribution, and the storage of. Food stuff, laundry stuff, petrol stuff and stuff to drink. It all fell within the Donner mandate. Fine goods or dry goods but mostly poker.

George's passion was poker. The straight goods. Followers of the Pin Main Saturday night game functioned as the DEW-line warrant officers. The ruling potentate. Those who must be obeyed and even they did not treat an invitation to join the game lightly.

George made several more calls and then, before the sun began its rapid plunge into Alaska, and the humid tanning salon reverted to a wooden meat freezer, George dressed and retired to his office to deal with the Friday details. There were always details to attend to as the Friday workday ended.

In Cam Main, Doc made arrangements for his weekend adventure, starting with the assembly of two thousand dollars, preferably in tens and twenties.

On Saturday morning, before daybreak, the Polar Aire crew were performing the DC-3 pre-flight checks. The Cam Main western flight was scheduled for departure at 0600 hours.

Doc, with five other suffering souls, had arrived at five thirty and each man displayed a severe early morning rumpled look. A pronounced case of cranky. They had been deposited in front of the airstrip's Quonset hut office and left to their own amusements in front of the locked reception-room door, their baggage in a heap on the gravel beside them. Shortly, while the men were still in a state of vocal numbness, the co-pilot appeared at the head of the boarding ramp and yelled, 'You passengers or what? Let's go.'

With no further announcement, the men boarded, the door closed and the Polar Aire flight departed the single, long, gravel strip heading west. At three thousand feet the captain leveled off. There would be three stops en-route to Pin Main and expected arrival at final destination was 1400 hours.

The skipper relaxed but shortly he asked the co-pilot for a fix.

'I want to check that gyrocompass bearing while we still have Venus.'

The co-pilot with charts, pocket watch and octant in hand, moved towards the tail section – the toilet, to be precise – where he could make stellar observations of the stars Arcturus, Dubhe and Sirus from the small Plexiglas window.

The winds were favorable with a twenty-knot tailwind. The pilot trimmed his ship, fine-tuning for a smoother flight. They had two hundred gallons of extra fuel on board, standard precautions in the Arctic. The forecast was for scattered cumulus cloud from an Alaskan system with turbulence at ten thousand feet. Their air speed would be one hundred and seventy miles an hour and they could expect to be on the ground at Pin Four by seven thirty. The captain tapped the pressure altimeter, confirming the stabilization of the instrument. He had zeroed it to a sea-level setting at Cam Main. Altimeters can be wrong by five hundred feet, or more, if not adjusted to the immediate local. In the distance, along the shoreline, what appeared to be seasonal, spring fog banks were forming.

The landing strip at Pin Four had been built on the side of a hill with large rock decorations on the bordering tundra that art gallery catalogues frequently described as Canadian primitive. An earthy panorama offering unique charm. Color had been splashed randomly in the form of broken airplanes, abandoned when they bent themselves around the rocks, or in the case of two aluminum remnants, failure to stop at the end of the runway.

The strip ran northwest to southeast and there was a three-degree incline. To land, a pilot sat the plane down at one hundred and ten miles per hour, flying uphill, past the decrepit airport waiting room. No brakes needed here because of the uphill incline and the usual prevailing twenty-knot offshore breeze. In a very short distance the express train speed was reduced to a modest ten knots for a turn around and return to waiting ground crew.

At seven fifty-five, the Polar Aire westbound flight was in takeoff position. The captain set the carburetor mixture and throttle and propeller controls for takeoff and the plane rolled forwards, uphill. The engines were pushed to full power, and when the ground speed was one hundred and twenty miles per hour, it became airborne and immediately turned westward.

The distance between Pin Four and Pin Three is one hundred and forty miles and from this, one thousand feet above sea level, the pilot almost expects to see the Pin Three billboard antennas. During the down time the weather had changed and fog banks towered to three thousand feet. The captain asked the co-pilot to call Lady Franklin Point to ask for an immediate weather update.

The reply was not promising. Visibility was dropping and there was now a five-hundred-feet ceiling with increasing fog patches reducing the airfield visibility to one mile. Better move your butt, boy.

The winds had increased from the north to thirty-five miles an hour which left the DC-3 plowing upstream. The pilot had to consider alternatives. Return to Cambridge Bay or continue on westward. They could ignore the landing strip at Lady Franklin Point and carry on to the civilian airport at Coppermine or fly even farther to Port Radium.

The captain had fuel reserves of two hundred gallons and some would say this was fat. This Arctic fog could dissipate as fast as it formed and if you are a good boy the tooth fairy will…

In fifty minutes they arrived at the fog bank that enfolded Pin Three. There was no point in further investigation because they were now flying through very wet stuff. A voice from the Coppermine weather station reported there was still time to find their runway and the prudent captain began to climb back into the sunshine and blue sky. The captain, decision made, informed the DOT at Cambridge Bay that they were flying to their alternate and requested clearance directly to Coppermine. They would be using one hundred and fifty gallons of fuel an hour and would arrive with ample reserves but, more importantly, before the fog.

Once again the winds increased and rather than scatter the fog banks, the perverse air movement moved the moist entity ashore, across the Coronation Gulf and up the river towards Coppermine. The first warning of major trouble was the loss of radio. The quiet of the headphones was replaced with a constant hiss.

There was a roughness in the air and the outside temperature was now an improbable twenty degrees, ideal for ice conditions. The co-pilot was instructed to tune the radio.

'Try to raise Cambridge Bay. Tell them about this new front.'

The radio was useless and the windshield had gradually fogged over and was now opaque. The pilot commanded that the de-icer be started. In the wings, rubber boots were activated and the pilot switched on the landing lights to observe the intermittent pulsations. The boots swelled and collapsed, breaking the sheets of ice into great flakes. Ice formed on the propeller hub and the smooth geometrical design gradually altered in shape, assuming a cow-patty blob configuration.

The plane shuddered from port to starboard, and again, like a dog shaking off the bath water. The propeller blades were accumulating ice and the delicate balance of these three-hundred-and-eighty-pound revolving wings was being disturbed. The pilot instructed the junior man to spray some de-icer on the props and the co-pilot, with great difficulty, operated a hand pump behind his seat. Beads of sweat formed on his forehead, not altogether from the hard work of manually pumping de-icer. The smell of alcohol filled the cabin and another shudder slithered across the plane but the de-icer helped. Golf ball-sized ice chunks began pummeling and banging the aluminum airship. The banging increased and the din became a roar.

The pilot had now entered into physical combat with the elements. The aircraft was his sword, his shield, and his skill with this armament would now decide this life and death contest. His being was focused on the control panel, the power of the engines and the response of the aircraft to his demands. Are the laws of flight a truism? There were thirty instruments reporting engine conditions and they were all demanding attention.

The pilot's focus was drawn to the airspeed indicator, which fluttered and had fallen off to one hundred and thirty miles an hour. He had not reduced power and only minutes before they had been cruising at one hundred and seventy. There must be no further loss of airspeed. Such a load of ice would crash the plane if the speed fell below one hundred. The altimeter was sinking. They were losing two hundred feet a minute and at that rate of descent, in fifteen minutes, they would be ten feet deep in water. The pilot pushed the propeller controls to full low pitch. Power, they must have power.

The pilot stamped on the rudder controls, to no avail, for they were frozen but the ailerons were free. They could still turn, slowly, gently, a few degrees only, for at this speed a turn could induce a spin from which there would be no recovery. And suddenly the number one engine was dead. For ten seconds. It surged into life and the pilot applied a full, rich mixture to the carburetor and worked the wobble pump, a manual pump for immediate fuel injection.

Number two engine now lost power and number one began to fade. This was not carburetor ice for the instrument panel check had verified that the carburetor heaters were on. Possibly magneto failure? No. One, but not both, and not together.

The pilot cut the fuel mixture to the number two, starving it, and it backfired. It belched a tongue of flame with an explosive bang and the pilot put the fuel mixture to full rich and the engine surged to full power. The co-pilot likened the full-throated roar to sonorous organ music. A heavenly choir. The pilot applied the same remedy to the number one engine and enjoyed similar success.

The pilot said, 'The ice is building up on the air intake manifolds. Getting a lot on the wings as well.'

He could see as much as two inches of ice building up on the wing edges causing more problems. The plane was flying at one hundred and twenty knots. Any less and it would not fly, not with the added weight of the ice and the ice was thickening as they watch.

The altimeter was dropping at the rate of two hundred feet a minute and in fifteen minutes, maybe less, the plane would be surfing with the icebergs. They were now eleven minutes from touchdown at Coppermine. The pilot would fly her straight in and, once committed, the pilot must land.

The ailerons were still free and the airship could be steered from side to side but, without lift, it is no longer a flying machine. The number one stalled again and again, the pilot starved it into submission and it returned to life with a roar and then number two demanded the pilot's attention. The engine was a dead thing for an infinite ten seconds, only to return to full power, surging and howling in protest with the propeller spinning towards oblivion, threatening to tear loose, until the pilot soothed the wildness.

They were now locked onto the Coppermine beacon and the radio roaring hiss had been replaced by normal silence. The pilot spoke to the Coppermine tower and they informed him that he was exactly on course.

'Come on in.'

Down a long glide through the swirls of fog and at last something besides white, fuzzy mist. At two hundred feet they broke through and the airplane touched down at one hundred and five miles an hour with full power, landing gear down and flaps that were working, because somebody up there likes DC-3s. The plane did not stall and nothing buckled and the plane rolled along the runway at a respectable eighty miles an hour. Miraculously the windshield cleared and at the terminal building the ground crew flagged them to a stop and waved both flags for a shut down.

The pilot complied, stretched and said, 'I believe I'll go to town for a beer.'

Doc spent several hours drinking stuff out of a Styrofoam cup and staring through dirt-encrusted windows. The view from all windows was the same, landscape that rivaled the DEW-line bleak moonscape, field and stream. The Saturday night game was becoming a might-have-been.

At 1300 hours, the airport staff had advised the waiting passengers that, 'This building will be closed at four o'clock. That is 1600 hours for you salty DEW-line types and there ain't nothing to eat here anyway.'

That was the last straw for the sour Mr. Rafferty. He conceded defeat and called a taxi. The game at Pin Main would have to wait. Doc was in an awkward position for he was not a passenger and Polar Aire was in no way responsible for his creature comforts. No meals, no room, no smiling face saying, 'Good afternoon, Mr. Rafferty. Welcome to the Purple Palace. We hope your stay with us will be a pleasant one.' Not for Doc but he did need food and lodging. Sustenance, as it were. What ho.

Twenty minutes after Doc's telephoned request for transportation, a battered, rusted fifty-five Buick arrived and shuddered to a stop at the waiting-room passenger door. Shortly a loud, breezy clamorous Inuit burst into the drab waiting room.

'Doc. Doc, you old piss head! By God damn it is you!' and Doc was scooped up. The Inuit whirled Doc around and yelled and only when he stopped did Doc realize who was assaulting him.

Doc grinned and said, 'Smiling Jack. It's you. Haven't seen you since Foxe.'

'Hey, Doc. How are you? I was told downtown that you are here, so I drop it all and hurry. You bet. So now I'm here with my new taxi machine.'

'Jack, I still have those slippers, my dog skin mukluks. The ones Jeannie made. How is Jeannie?'

'Okay, all okay. We better go downtown. You eat? I fix everything. Food, room. You want a bottle? Good stuff.'

After registration and coughing up the room deposit at the hotel and after a steak and beer lunch at the Elks and after the preparation and lighting of a three-dollar cigar, Doc smiled. A big full-faced smile, the first of the day. Happy was still with him.

'You bought yourself a taxi?'

'Damn "A". I'm the taxi driver. I own the car and the taxi sign and now, I'm a damned good driver. Making lots of bucks. Me and Jeannie. She answers the phone and has babies. Three, maybe next year be four.'

'So tell me, Jack. What's the big deal in this town?'

'Gold. Gold mines, Doc. Lots of gold and silver. Big mines and big money.'

'Ah, sure, now I remember… Patricia Silver. Gold mine listed on the Toronto Exchange. Right, and another one called Bad Boy Resources. Big stuff but not for me. My game is poker. You remember Jack, a thinking man's pastime.'

'What I hear, Doc, a lot of politicians play poker.'

'Well, Eisenhower does and Truman did. Both good men.'

'Sure. Good men. Ho, boy, who you kid? Anyway, I can get you a game right here. A private game here in the club. Give me a minute. I'll talk to the manager. Guy named Paul Johnson. I'll be right back.'

The Inuit left Doc sitting, contemplating the remnants of the steak and enjoying the after-dinner cigar, a picture of expansive content.

In a very short time Jack returned accompanied by a tall, solidly build, balding person who greeted Doc.

'Hi, I'm Paul Johnson and I already know your name. Heard about the Foxe slot car races and today we meet the maestro in person. Welcome, Doc. Heard about the flight in. You must be wearing horseshoes or maybe it's leprechauns, with a name like Rafferty.'

'I'll tell the world and we had a pilot and a half flying today. There was four inches of ice on sections of the wings. And now, seeing that the Gods are being so kind, I thought I might play a bit of poker.'

'Saturday afternoon, some of the members play some seven card stud. I should warn you, it's poker. They expect five hundred up front, table stakes and a five-dollar limit. It's for the big boys. Not much spit in the ocean or fiery cross.'

'Sounds all right to me. Give me a minute to clean up.'

When Doc returned to the dining room Happy Jack excused himself.

'I gotta go now, Doc. Work a little or Jeannie yell lots. I'll come back in a couple of hours.'

Paul accompanied Doc and made introductions to the seated players. Doc noted a Rolex watch and one guy with a large diamond pinkie ring. Definitely poker players. The men nodded as Doc was introduced. One skinny grease ball said something about, 'Don't need no railbirds. You one of them Edmonton wannabe high rollers?'

'Not me, bud.'

Doc took his seat and flattened out fifty twenty-dollar bills. They made a nice pile. Thick. Impressive. The Rolex watch straightened up and arranged his chair, moving closer to the table. Somebody else remarked, 'I've always liked a Saturday pay day.'

Doc smiled at the table, and the dealer said, 'Very well, gentlemen, ante up,' and dealt the players two cards down.

Doc was sitting three players to the left of the dealer, holding an ace and ten of spades. The bet came to him and he laid out twenty bucks and three players folded. The Rolex called, as did the dealer and a guy in a plaid shirt.

The first flip card gave Doc a six of spades and he checked to the dealer. A ten of hearts and four of spades left Doc with a pair and fifty bucks in the pot and Rolex was sitting with queens. Everyone else had folded. Doc raised ten dollars to the queens. Doc and Rolex checked to the sixth card.

The last card was dealt and Doc peeked at his last face down and then raised ten bucks after the 'queens' bet twenty. The 'queens' called and rolled the third queen and embarrassed Doc and his three tens. It might be a long evening.

At 1500 hours, Doc was acclimatized. He had noted some of the players give away signs, some of their mannerisms. He was down a hundred but, what the hell, call it the initiation fee. Now, he was on his way. It was a big surprise to see the Polar Aire co-pilot standing in the doorway with Happy Jack fluttering in the background. Jack shrugged his shoulders and his facial expression as much as said, 'Sorry, but what can I do?'

The co-pilot was brusque.

'Been looking all over hell for you. We're leaving. The captain is flying out as fast as we get you on board. DOT approved our takeoff at 1530 hours. The weather has cleared and the ground crew have knocked the ice off our bird and we're headed home. Let's go.'

Doc was in a dismal frame of mind on the way to the airport. Happy Jack repeated over and over how sorry he was.

'Jeannie is real sorry. She was cooking a big supper. She wanted you to meet Lettie. A damned nice girl. Jeanie's sister who is built, oh boy, is she built. How the hell did I know this guy want to fly? He said we got to find you. Okay?'

'Sure. Next time, I'll stay longer. Make a night of it. Let's keep in touch. Let me know about any gold mines?'

At 1550 hours, the blue and white DC-3 lifted off from the Coppermine International and headed east. Two hours later the plane landed at Cambridge Bay after a routine flight. They rolled to a stop at the hangar with all systems normal.

Doc had slept for the past hour and now suffered a dry mouth and a slight headache, which he attributed to the incessant roar of the Pratt and Whitney engines. He stopped to thank the flight crew and added, 'Polar Aire should add a stewardess and champagne for these Saturday adventure junkets.'

Monday morning George Donner phoned Doc.

'Hear you flew all over the north.'

'Partly, George, partly. We did see some different country. Sorry I missed your game.'

'That's why I'm calling. How about next Saturday?'

'Thanks, George, but I have a couple of other things to look after. But while I have you on the line, I ran into some interesting information about gold mines. The ground floor with regards to some property in the Coppermine area.'

Chapter Twenty

Aaron and Doc spent long hours arranging the itinerary of their R and R. Twenty-seven days of fun in the sun, and a major concern was that there be a minimum of time wasted traveling. Bad enough was the time consumed, sitting in airplanes, but the barren hours squandered in airports could only lead to a life of drink.

The final arrangements were such that they would overnight in Winnipeg for a spot of climatic exposure, so to speak, and then a direct flight to London. London, England. A great place for variety. Smooth, gorgeous, compliant women, great beer and very sophisticated clubs. So it might cost a buck or two. The English entertained with verve and they did screw with style.

A short flight to Copenhagen for breakfast and then, for tanning purposes only, five days in Monte Carlo. 'Remember that is a pebble beach, old sock?' Well, maybe some baccarat, or a few bob on the wheel and then a direct flight from Paris would have them back in Winnipeg with six hours to spare before check-in at Hangar Nine.

They arose at an early hour, completed the packing of their travel kits, had some breakfast and arrived at the airport ahead of schedule.

Doc, with some pomposity, said to Aaron, 'A well-organized person is rarely subject to the mundane inconveniences.'

They boarded and strapped themselves into their assigned seats. For the next half an hour they sat and smiled at each other and, with fellow passengers, laughed uproariously at old jokes. Eventually, they taxied down the runway and headed southward. Doc began preparing a forbidden cigar for the purpose of inhalation.

Aaron nudged him and said, 'I suffered my yearly fumigation last week. You don't have to light that thing on my account.'

Doc gave Aaron a big grin and put the black cigar away.

There was a quiet period before Aaron asked Doc, 'Are you ever going to explain what went wrong with that doll in Toronto?'

There was a pause before Doc replied, 'You mean that redhead? The bouncy thing you thought was so great?'

'You thought so too but you've never mentioned her. I would have bet that one rated another outing.'

'No way, Aaron, no way. That bundle of delight lowered my ego by twenty points. Mind you, she was choice, prime stuff but... Well, what happened. We wined, dined, made stimulating conversation, blew in each other's ears and in due course made our way back to her place. The evening progressed as planned and eventually we were cavorting nude between the sheets. I had just made my penetration when she mumbled something or other. I said, "What is it, darling?", and she said, "Are you in, ducks?" Well, hell, my lance collapsed like a noddle in hot water.'

Aaron's face was red and tears of laughter were trickling down his cheeks. In a choked voice he asked, 'What did you say?'

'Say! Say? What could I say? I asked her, was it as great for you as it was for me, lover? So, the long and short, I don't think I'll call that one again.'

Aaron was still doubled over with laughter when the stewardess made an appearance. The coffee-serving lady was a Christmas morning, tinsel-wrapped package for the horny DEW-liners. She was dressed in a blue uniform, blue pillbox hat, short blue jacket, white blouse and snug blue skirt that started about two inches above her lovely knees. Petite blue shoes that supported marvelous nylon-clad, upward-flowing legs. She smiled and exchanged small pleasantries as she progressed down the aisle dispensing coffee and plastic packaged cookies. A relatively tall girl, five foot six or seven, with short wavy brown hair and thick-lashed brown eyes. A lively, provocative, saucy lady.

Tousled heads popped up from between the seats like a colony of ground squirrels. Men were dozing, awoke puzzled, and then with the realization that it was a female scent, their heads snapped up, their gaze zeroed in and locked on, heads swiveling, following her every move.

Each man in turn made some unintelligible reply to her query about coffee, tea, or juice and when she moved on past, they twisted around in the seat, following her sway, stop, bend and swirl dance down the aisle. Aaron and Doc were sitting bolt upright for a better view and whilst the goddess was still two seats away, Doc announced to Aaron that he was in love.

'This is the real thing.'

Aaron, who was leaning out into the aisle, answered, 'I hope it's not the girl I'm taking home to meet Mother.'

When the vision arrived at their seat she leaned across Aaron to pour Doc's coffee. The girl was inches away. Her warm scent, the rustle of nylon, perhaps an unconscious psyche, perhaps a Freudian devil that besets the pursuing male, overcame Aaron. There was no rational explanation for Aaron's out-of-character direct approach. He coughed to gain her attention and when the girl turned her head, her brown eyes now mere inches away, Aaron, with his gaze riveted down past the open blouse button into the deep forbidden crevice, said, 'Miss, would you bring those beautiful breasts to breakfast?'

The gorgeous red mouth flew open, exposing the small pink tongue. The comely young lady leapt like a deer backwards and up, away from the unswerving gaze focused on the partly open blouse. Her head bashed against the curved, overhead baggage compartment and the hand-held coffee pot drooped. Brown, steaming fluid poured into Doc's lap. Doc's glasses bounced to the end of his nose. He arched backwards, his torso twisting away from the stream of coffee but to no avail. The pot was emptied into Doc's now soggy trousers. The girl was frozen with a stricken look on her face. The coffee pot hung over Doc. One last drop plopped into the puddle before the girl fled up the aisle.

Aaron pulled himself out of his seat and turned to help Doc, who was pulling at the top of his trousers, and trying to undo the fly. He yanked at the coffee-soaked shirt, trying to get the tail out of his trousers, and when this effort proved too slow, he stood up, letting them fall to his knees. Then, embarrassed by the circle of anxious faces gathered to help, he sat with his trousers draped around his ankles. Aaron arrived with a wad of toilet tissue which he dumped in his lap, and Doc, very timidly, began patting at his wet boxer shorts.

'I'm ruined. She's destroyed me.'

Aaron was about to reply when the stewardess pushed through the circle of men and poured a pitcher of water onto Doc's lap. Doc's yell would have stopped a charging bull. Aaron grabbed the girl and swung her away from Doc.

'Are you crazy?'

'No, no, cold water. It's a treatment for burns… really.'

Aaron held her by the shoulders and looked at Doc, who was ineffectively dabbing at his red and white polka dot shorts with a handful of soggy tissue paper.

The girl said, 'I can help. The cold water and now a cold compress. I have towels,' and Aaron reluctantly released her.

She knelt down beside Doc's bare knees and began patting at the burned area. Shortly, Doc gave a small grin and said something like, 'There, there, my dear.'

The girl appeared not to hear him, but then suddenly her face turned a bright red. She straightened up and with a slight quiver in her voice said to Aaron, 'Your friend will recover. I'm very sorry about his shirt. I'll pay to have it cleaned,' and she wheeled around and fled up the aisle.

Aaron, with a puzzled look, watched her go and then turned to Doc who had produced a cigar and now sat with legs widespread, preparing it for smoking. The front of his coffee-stained shorts bulged dramatically with the effort of containing Doc's erection. He grinned at Aaron and said, 'It seems that I'm not destroyed.'

Without further mishap, and incidentally, no reappearance of the goddess of health, 'Salus', Doc had supplied the sobriquet.

The plane landed in Winnipeg and the men hurried to the Carlton Hotel to claim reserved rooms. Aaron, with Doc hobbling slowly behind, made his way through the chrome and glass lobby, much like a pilgrim newly arrived in Mecca. At the reservation desk, Dave Inglis, the assistant manager, greeted them with instant recognition and loud howdies.

'You made it. I heard you were here but that there had been an accident… That Doc had to go to the hospital. Half a dozen guys have checked in and they all said the same thing. What happened?'

Doc raised a hand and said, 'First the room. I need a long, cool tub… and ointment. No, I need ointments; internal and external. Aaron will supply you with the details of my misadventure. What about you, Dave? How have you been? How are the wife and kids? But tell me later. Right now I need treatment.'

Dave said, 'I'll get some ointment and be right up.' He handed Doc a room key. Doc checked the number and smiled.

'Room 407, my lucky room number.' Over his shoulder, on the way to the elevator, he added, 'Thank you.'

Before the elevator doors closed, Dave called, 'Your internal ointment, Doc. It's on the coffee table. The usual brand.'

'Thanks, Dave.' Doc held the door open momentarily and said, 'Aaron, come by for a drink when you're cleaned up. We'll see what we do after I've checked these burns.'

Aaron took time to explain Doc's condition and exchange pleasantries and it was an hour before he knocked at the ajar Room 407 door. Doc yelled something and then yelled something else. Aaron found Doc, beaming, sitting in the center of a sunken marble bathtub. The bathtub's gold-colored taps and faucet were miniature lion heads. The apron was tiled in royal blue. Wall to wall broadloom covered the remaining floor area. Double marble sinks lined one wall and were complemented by a full-length dressing table opposite. Inset in the ceiling was a heat lamp and exhaust fan and spaced between these were grill-covered speakers from which strains of Montevani's violins played softly. A touch of reality was the wall-mounted dark-blue telephone.

'Aaron, old buddy, is this a great watering hole or is this a great watering hole? Grab a glass. I've got the bottle here.'

'You look like you've arrived. How are you, Doc? How are the burns?'

'This water business really helps. I wouldn't have believed it but, Christ, when I got out of my clothes there were red and white swellings covering my whole belly and down to my nuts... but this treatment, take a look.'

Like Triton arising from the Aegean Sea, Doc stood with the water pouring off his pelt. The only evidence of the mishap were white blistered blotches, none of any size.

'That's great, Doc. I'm glad you're okay.'

'Okay. Hell, in another hour I'll be back to perfect. Where's your drink? What's happening tonight?'

Aaron unwrapped a sanitized packaged glass and poured from Doc's handy-to-the-tub bottle. 'I'm not sure about tonight. I'm looking at a couple of things but what about you? Are you going to be fit to travel tomorrow?'

'Hey, Aaron. It's me. I'll be all right.'

'Good. I figured I might drop downstairs to the bar for a drink with Rocky. See how he is. Oh hell… I might as well tell you. I got her number this afternoon and I figured I'd better phone her. Reassure her about your health… you know.'

'Don't worry about me, Aaron. The awkward dame with her coffee pot did me a favor.' Doc lifted his glass and continued, 'For six months I've had a recurring dream. Something about a bathtub. And look at this, you could drown an alligator in this thing.'

Aaron nodded his head in agreement. He spent a short time admiring the decor before raising his glass.

'We of the proletariat salute you, Caesar. This edifice is worthy of your presence.'

Doc smiled. 'Yes indeed, Aaron, that's aptly put. I feel that with such accommodation, I should indulge myself; soak and sip. Enjoy the bounty.'

'I don't blame you, Doc. It's really something, but I'm heading for the bar and unless things change I'll see you in the morning maybe. Who knows? I'll look in when I get back.'

'What time in the morning?'

'Check-in at the airport at seven thirty. Okay?'

'Okay.' Doc waved him away. 'See you in the morning.'

Doc topped up his drink, ran some hot water and then lay back with a small sigh, contemplating his navel, so to speak. At 8:00 P.M., the silence of the long multi-door hotel hallway was disturbed by Amy Ingakik knocking on the door of Room 407. Again she knocked and after a brief wait she used her passkey and entered.

Amy was the hotel's house matron and during the evening she checked each registered room to ensure that there were no discrepancies in the room's furnishings. She would turn back a corner of the bedspread, leave a chocolate on the pillow, adjust the thermostat, clean ashtrays, deposit clean glasses and, before leaving, turn on a reading lamp – all the small stagings that instill a sense of homeliness into a somber hotel-room atmosphere.

Amy was pulling the full-length drapes closed when a voice from the open bathroom door asked, 'Is that you, Aaron?'

'Pardon me, sir. I'm the maid. I'm checking that your room is comfortable.'

'Thank God. Ah... Miss... Miss... Would you come here, please?'

'What is it you wish, sir? Towels, soap? I can leave fresh towels on the bed.'

'No, no. I need some help. Please, Miss. Will you call the front desk? I need a plumber... right now. I'm stuck and I need a plumber.'

Amy tentatively peeked around the doorway and gasped and then, in the polite manner of the Inuit, quickly hid a full smile in the palm of her hand. Doc's head stuck up above the blue-tiled bathtub rim and Doc's foot was equally high above the bath, held there by Doc's big toe which was stuck or was being swallowed by the gold-colored lion's head sculptured tap. The portion of the toe that was visible was white, pasty white, as was the foot, the ankle and Doc's drooping head.

'My goodness. What are you doing?'

Doc's head popped up, and as the girl moved forwards into the room, he murmured a fervent, 'Thank God. The cavalry has arrived. Miss, if you would be so kind. I find that my toe is stuck, my leg has turned to ice and I'm out of whisky. If you would phone the front desk and have a bottle... and a plumber... Right away. Please?'

Amy moved farther into the marble room, and asked, 'What is it? Are you cold?'

Doc had begun to shiver, and was visibly shaking, and the girl, seeing this, grabbed up a large bath towel and draped it around his shoulders. When she saw the white and pink burns on Doc's stomach, groin and thighs, she frowned with concern.

'Have you been sitting here long? What caused you to do such a thing? What has happened to you?'

Doc levered himself into a more upright position, and bashfully attempted a covering with a small sponge.

'First, dear lady, a plumber. I need my toe extracted. Please.'

Ignoring the plea, Amy knelt at the tap and began to rub the sickly white foot and said, 'We must get some blood moving to this foot. It is a very bad thing, Doc. Very bad.'

Shortly Doc said, 'It is feeling prickly, like fire. Thank you. You know my name. Do I know you?'

'Yes, or at least my brother, Sammy at Hall Beach. I'm Amy Ingakik.'

Doc's mouth fell open, and he stared at the black-haired woman and then he remembered. 'Amy… Amy, what the hell is a nice girl…? No, no, I mean, Amy, you were seventeen at the Christmas party last year. No, two years ago. What the hell? What are you doing here?'

'It was three years ago, and I work here as the night maid. I've been here a year. Since I finished school. I'm sorry, Doc. I'm not going to get this toe out, but if I call the front desk you're going to be embarrassed.'

'Oh hell, you're right. Let me think. Would you get me a blanket? I'm still freezing.'

'What happened to your stomach? That looks sore. Are they burns?'

Not waiting for a reply, Amy hurried out and shortly she was back with a blanket and a pillow and proceeded to make Doc more comfortable.

'Amy, call down and see if Dave is still around. He'll know what to do, and then call the bar. Ask Rocky to send up a bottle.'

Dave had left the hotel at eight, but Dorothy, the girl on the desk, thought he would be back before midnight, maybe at eleven. He often came in on his way home.

'Have him call Room 407, please. It's urgent. Have him call, no matter what the time.' Amy hung up the bathroom convenience phone. 'Oh, Doc. You look so pathetic. What can I do for you?'

Amy was a vivacious, four-foot, ten-inch, well-developed woman. The pageboy cut of her jet black hair framed the delightful saucy smile and the twinkling happy eyes.

During the next several hours, she was an attentive listener to Doc's narrative, shyly laughing at the humor, agreeing with some of his logic, and occasionally correcting misconceptions about women and/or Inuit lifestyle. Doc increasingly realized what a treasure had come to him. This handsome intelligent woman was as attuned to Doc as he was to her. By slow degrees he lapsed into silence and sat captivated, smiling. The demands of the long day called for payment and he slept. The lady from Hall Beach sat stroking his soft hair back away from his closed eyes.

At ten thirty, Dave received the message to call Room 407. It was late, but then remembering the burns Doc was suffering, he was soon standing beside Amy, looking down at the sleeping Doc.

'How the hell did he get his toe in there?' The assistant manager had kept his voice to what he thought was a low level, but Doc stirred and opened one eye.

'You never got stuck in the wrong hole?' Doc asked. 'Good to see you, Dave. You know Amy? Right, of course you do. Sorry to bother you at this time of night, but you're here now and what are you going to do about getting this trap off my foot?'

'I have a problem, Doc. That piece of pipe has a six-hundred-dollar replacement value plus the cost of a plumber.'

'Dave, you might have to pay triple time and there is going to be some banging and hammering which might disturb other guests, but, well, Dave, I don't give a shit.'

'I have to consider the various aspects, Doc.'

'You want me to sue? The hotel is responsible for room furnishings and this furnishing has proven unsafe... And shove your six hundred. You think you can leave me here as curiosity for future guests when they are having consumptive problems? Get me out of this, Dave. God damn it, I'm cold, my ass hurts, my back aches, and my toe is dead and I haven't eaten for twenty hours... And you stand there yapping about the price of a hunk of bathroom pipe.'

'I'm sorry, Doc. You're right. We'll have you out in a jiffy.'

Dave departed in a rush and Doc grinned at Amy.

'Which reminds me, let's get some food. What would you like? A steak... or maybe a sandwich? Say, how about some Chinese? Sure, that's it. Do that will you, Amy? Phone the Polynesian Room and order up some Chinese.'

Amy was still on the phone when Dave returned with a bag of tools and proceeded with the destruction of the toe-stuffed tap. Before midnight, Doc and Amy were enjoying a Polynesian feast presented by the now compliant assistant manager. Dave stayed for a nightcap and Sharkey, Norm and Ed dropped in when they heard in the bar that Doc was having a party.

In the small hours the last of the unexpected and uninvited guests departed, including Dave and his bag of tools. The door to Room 407 was still open when Aaron arrived.

A boisterous, 'Come in, come in,' command to enter surprised Aaron but the state of Doc's room was a shock.

'You must have had one hell of a party.'

'The neighbors from 405 and 409 and a few of the boys. Amy, may I present my good buddy, Aaron Dempster. Aaron, I'm glad you're here because things have changed. Some slight adjustments to our itinerary. Not entirely of my choosing. Circumstances have ah… Do you remember Sharkey? Small guy. Radician at Pin Three.'

'Sure. He was a year behind us at Streator. Ex-navy type.'

'That's him. What do you think of him?'

'He's okay, Doc, not bad, but I've only met him a couple of times.'

'Like I said, he was here for a while. Norm and Ed were with him but anyway, Sharkey is on some R and R and he's looking at Europe. Hell, the long and short of it is, what about taking him to London?'

'Well, ah, well. How do you feel about it, Doc? Can he get tickets at this late date? We have a tight schedule.'

'The thing is, Aaron, I'd sell him mine. There are matters here in the 'Peg' that require my immediate attention, and I confess, I don't feel as mobile as I did twelve hours ago.' Doc continued. 'As a matter of fact I feel a bit worn. Used up, as it were.'

'Well, shit, Doc. Those burns will heal. A week and they won't be much other than scars.'

'What you say is true, but what about this?'

Doc, who was seated on the floor for easier availability to the food, raised his right foot above the clutter of Chinese take-out food cartons. The now swollen, red and purple member that was a foot rose into view.

Aaron gasped before taking a long drink and asked, 'What the hell have you been doing?'

Doc skipped a lengthy explanation with, 'No big deal, but I'm going to have trouble walking, so it occurred to me that rather than screw up your R and R, take Sharkey.' He continued with the persuasion, 'There'll be some laughs, and Sharkey pays his way. Nothing cheap about him and he enjoys a glass of bubbly. Like you say, he's not bad.'

'What about you, Doc? What happened to your foot?'

'Not to worry, Aaron.' Doc looked to Amy and, reassured, continued. 'Not to worry. There are events that beset a man on his journey through life; trials and testing periods that we must rise above. As I have often said, a well-organized person is rarely subject to the mundane inconveniences, but I digress. What's happening here is, Dave, a true gentleman, has released Amy from current duties so that she might act in the capacity of a nursing companion.' Doc gave Amy a big smile. 'With such a lovely associate, I have no doubt that this will be a memorable R and R.'

Aaron snorted and grinned, then finished his drink and said, 'I've got an early start. Anything you want from Europe? Nothing! Then I'll see you in three weeks. Take care of yourself, Doc. Get him into a body cast, Amy. That may save you. Goodnight.'

The moon hung around, hovering in the southern sky for another hour and then it too departed. Doc chuckled, Amy giggled and they talked away the last hours before morning.

Chapter Twenty-One

The lounge was a bright, sunlit spacious comfort place when Aaron arrived and took a table beside the thirty-foot-high view window that overlooked the airport loading ramp. During his patient wait, the lounge area became a place of discreet lamps and blue shadows. Below him, men in white overalls drove long tractor-trailer loads of luggage through cones of light to parked airplanes. Occasionally, he checked the time and signaled the saucy blonde waitress for another drink, but his attention remained focused on the service activities being performed on the arriving and departing silver-skinned aircraft.

He greeted the overdue Doc with a smile of relief and a 'Where the hell have you been?'

'Traffic, old buddy, traffic, cars and people. You been waiting long? I'm sorry. Jeez, Aaron, but you are a sight for sore eyes.'

'How is my married friend. You're looking successful, Mr. Rafferty. Amy is feeding you a lot of donuts or what?'

'How are you, Aaron? Good to see you too. About this expanded waistline, I do a lot of brain stuff. Deep thinking and what happens then is…'

'Doc, you still have a great gift of the gab. It's been too long. Too damn long but enough of the chitchat. You missed the first round and you can catch up by buying the next one.'

'That's a deal. How long have you been waiting?'

'I had nothing else to do and I needed a touch of civilized drinking but in another twenty minutes, I think I could talk that waitress into spending a week at Saint Croix.'

'You're suffering from green grass fever and the smell of that French oil tank farm won't help.'

'Maybe, maybe not, but I do need some palm trees and grass skirts.'

The drinks arrived but it was several minutes before Doc said to his friend, 'You're getting too old for that Hula-hula bullshit.'

'You heard of something better?'

'You know what I mean.'

They sat in silence, tasting the newly arrived drinks. Doc broke the awkward time.

'I'm sorry about being late. I had more running around than I figured on. You know what I mean. Driving around, looking for a parking space. This damned town. Every day it gets worse.'

'How are things otherwise, Doc? How do you like cooking hamburgers?'

'This franchise business is more than cooking, old buddy. Like I was saying, it takes a lot of running around, picking up supplies, picking up laundry and running to the bank and the damned traffic! Then there's the cleaning. Clean the grill, clean the deep fryer, clean the john. A glorified janitor who fills in government forms, that's me.'

'You making any money?'

'Aaron, I've made more money this past six months than I made in the last two years I worked on the line, but damn me, do I work for it. Six in the morning to midnight, seven days a week. There are a lot of times when I miss that twice a month pay day.'

'Sure you do, Doc. You miss the icebergs too. Right?'

'Well, there are compensations. What about you? Where are you going? Where's the restoration and relaxing destination this time?'

'I've resigned. Handed in my quit notice, so it's not exactly R and R.'

The news startled Doc. He took a drink and then confirmed his friend's statement.

'You? You pulled the plug?'

'Ya. Enough is enough and I need a change. It's not the same DEW-line. Longer shifts, the food is all beginning to taste the same. They're paying more but it's getting bloody monotonous. I'm not alone. I talked to Michael last week. Spoke to both Michael and Jake. They should be here soon.' Aaron paused to check the time and continued, 'If that Polar Aire flight from Foxe is on time. But anyway, I talked to Michael and it sounded like he was headed elsewhere. Him and Jake. They feel the same, and as for me, well. The thing is, Doc, you were ahead of us. You made the right move six months ago.'

'I was lucky. If that "A and W" deal had been a week later, I would have been at Cam Main and it would have been damned hard to negotiate my franchise long-distance.'

The waitress appeared at the table, and said, 'A message for you or at least I think it's for you. Are you Doc?'

'That's me.'

'Someone called Michael. He and Jake are at Hangar Nine and want you to wait no more than half an hour.'

'Great. Thanks, doll. Bring us another round please and add two rye and water. VO, no ice. Okay?' Turning back to Aaron, Doc asked, 'So what do you have lined up? You got something to go to?'

'Ya, as a matter of fact, but wait a few minutes. I want Jake and Michael to hear it. But tell me about married life. How's Amy?'

'Great. She's raising chickens.'

'That's a twist. She raises them and you fry them.'

'No bloody way. The chickens she raises become her personal nursery. You know her. The way the Inuit kids grow up. No pets. Animals were eaten, even the dogs when there was nothing else. Well, all of a sudden, Amy's surrounded by small fluffy, yellow bundles that chirp, chirp, chirp along behind her wherever she goes.'

'You're kidding, Doc. I thought an Inuit would be the last one to forget what animals and fish are for.'

'Believe me. They have a screw loose about what they see as cruelty. Hey, here's Michael and Jake. Hi, big guy. How the hell are you? Hi, Michael, old buddy. What have they been feeding you? Double portions?'

'Hi, Doc. How's it hanging, Aaron?'

The banalities flew back and forth but slowly conversation wound down. Before the silence became awkward, four glasses were raised, drunk and thumped down, empty. The waitress was efficient and new drinks were shortly on the table.

Jake nodded at Aaron and asked, 'What's this I hear about you deserting the north?'

'You hear right.'

Michael laughed and said, 'Not you, Aaron. Haven't you heard? There's something about the north that gets in your blood.'

The three men looked at him in mock amazement, and then in unison chanted, 'There is something about the north that gets in your blood…' A dramatic pause, and then a very loud, '*Ice*.'

Michael nodded his head and then in falsetto voice said, 'You heard that one. Right, then how about the— '

All three – Doc, Jake and Aaron – interrupted with, 'We have heard that one too.'

When the laughter quieted down, Aaron said, 'Doc was telling me about his chicken farm. Amy won't let him fry them.'

Jake asked, 'That right, Doc?'

'Ya, something like that. The original plan with the acreage was to raise chickens and when they were ready I could use them at the restaurant. It would be something for Amy, some money of her own. We planned to feed about two thousand chickens and we spent a lot of time installing water troughs, auto-feeders, heaters, fans and control devices.' Doc took a drink and continued. 'After that job, I think Amy could have written an industrial control ticket and passed. Anyway, the chicks, about a thousand ounces of yellow fluff, arrived and we turned them loose in the super-controlled environment. We sat back and prepared to measure and record growth rate.

'About a week later, around midnight, the Manitoba Hydro goes out of business for five hours. Amy kicks me out of bed, and we start packing chicks into our oil-heated home. At five in the morning, the power came back on and our new house looks like an abandoned Puffin bird-nesting ground. You know what I mean? You've seen pictures in the *National Geographic*. Big black hunk of rock sticking up out of the surf, covered from top to bottom with white bird shit.'

Jake and Aaron were red-faced, choking with laughter. Michael sat with his mouth open, staring in disbelief.

Michael was quiet for a minute but then asked, 'You took all those chicks into the house? My God, Doc, what were you thinking of?'

'That's what I was saying in the morning. It was obvious that Amy and I were living in the wrong shelter. It took four days to wash down and shovel out and Amy… Well, what happened was that those chicks took to following her around. Everywhere: long yellow lines, chirping and running along behind. She tried hiding in the house and there would be this mob of chicks crowding up around the doors waiting for her to come out.'

'Why didn't you just lock them back up in the coop?'

'Nope. Amy wouldn't have it. Said they would adjust to the weather but if we provided protection and failed we would be murderers. Well, that was four months ago.'

'So you're out of the chicken business?'

'Ya. As a commercial enterprise, but we sure got a lot of pets. I tried taking some into town. I made a deal to have two hundred butchered, cleaned and plucked. Well, I had to release them. It turned out that Amy knew half of them personally, old friends, as it were. Now I feed them once a day and pray for foxes. Bound to be foxes showing up any day now and the price of fox skin is real good this year.'

They roared with laughter. The laughter was infectious and the waitress appeared and restored a degree of normalcy. 'You guys all right?'

Aaron grinned at her and said, 'Sure, darling, bring a round. Start drinking, guys. I'm an hour away from flying.'

The smile on Jake's face collapsed and he said, 'You made up your mind? You're going to Nam?'

'Aw hell, Jake. Just to check it out. It might be a year or two before they get serious about shooting Canadians.'

Doc said, 'It's hard to see a difference. Americans, Canadians, all the same hair-cut, old buddy.'

'Come off it, Doc. They're not interested in shooting Canadian civilians, and there's all them palm trees and white beaches. Any way you look, it's a lot better than a thousand miles of ice.'

Michael and Jake squirmed and looked away, staring into the now black night sky.

Doc, all laughter gone, said, 'You know that deal stinks. If you only believe one percent of the news reports the deal sucks. It's political and not even Canadian politics.'

Aaron stared down at his drink, pushing the glass in small circles and Doc glared.

Michael eased the tension with, 'Hey now. I heard a new one.' Jake looked at him expectantly. Aaron tried a grin and slowly Doc's tension faded.

They sat patiently, and at last Doc asked, 'So what is it?'

'It will come. Give me a minute.'

Doc slapped the table and roared, 'Michael, you're a royal pain in the ass. You just screwed up a great discourse on the twentieth-century moral conscience. With people like you around, it's no wonder we got such super halfwits in Ottawa. I tell you, it's bloody frustrating and some days I'd like to kick some ass. In some ways I'm lucky to have a nincompoop accountant because I can yell at him for five minutes and release a two-week head of steam.'

'Aaron's not the only one, Doc. I've been thinking about those Pacific breezes myself.'

'For Christ's sake, Jake! Not you? You're a big boy now.'

'Sure, Doc, but I need a change. I'm tired of watching the start of the next ice age. I want to whistle at a dame who isn't wearing forty pounds of caribou skins for a new summer dress. How about you, Michael? You coming to Washington? Page Electric is screaming for Troppo techs.'

'I heard about it, Jake, but it's not for me. Nope. I'm flying out...' and Michael checked his wristwatch, 'in twenty-eight minutes. I've enrolled at Simon Fraser, a university, a BC (British Columbia) university. I figured that I need some polish. After living with you uncouth bastards for five years, I need some culture. Some intellectual stimuli.'

'Hold it right there, Mister.' Jake, head thrust forward, glowered in mock rage at his friend. 'Hold it, you ugly little twerp. Where do you get off saying stuff about my couth. I'll bet you fifty bucks that I'm more couth than anyone at this table. I got couth I haven't even used. I read a book about couth, buddy.'

'You're uncouth, Jake. Nothing personal, but I can prove it. The waitress, an impartial observer, can render an unbiased judgment. Miss? Miss? A moment, please. May I call you dear? No? Well, in any case, this,' Michael pointed at Jake, 'this Neanderthal ape feels... no believes, that he possesses some modicum of good breeding, some degree of couth. Would you enlighten him?'

'Did you guys want another round? Otherwise I got people waiting. I haven't got time for this bullshit.'

'Thank you, Miss. Another round, please. Well, Jake? Do you agree?'

'Agree? Agree to what? Tell you what, I'll prove my superior couth by buying the next round.'

'If you're prepared to do that, I might concede. Perhaps I have been wrong, but this generosity does not detract from the basic premise that I have suffered five years in an intellectual vacuum.'

'Michael, do us a favor and shut up. At times your dialogue would gag a maggot and what do we need couth for? We got money.' Doc raised his glass and Aaron and Jake were quick to follow. 'To you, Michael. Good luck. That's a tough job you're moving into, going back to school. I don't envy you.'

'Thanks, Doc. If I flunk out, I'll be calling you for a job.'

'Do that. I can always use a good chicken-plucker with couth.'

First Aaron and Michael, then Doc and finally Jake, piled hand on hand in the center of the table. A group handshake.

Aaron said, 'We'd better get serious about the drinking. That was the Vancouver flight they just called.'

Michael grinned at his friends and then spent several moments studying the wet tracings his glass had made on the polished tabletop.

When he did look up, he said, 'Jake… I wish ah… what I mean… Look, keep in touch. Aaron, Doc, if there is ever anything… well, you know.'

'Save it, Michael. When you remember the end of that story, or any old punch line, write me. Even if you don't remember, drop me a line.'

Smiles were tight, and Michael, without further words, got up and left. The three sat for a minute watching the busy airport personnel below them, and at last Aaron raised his empty glass, summoning the busy waitress.

'Another round? How about your friend? Will he be back?'

'Not tonight, honey. So Jake. What about it? Will he make it?'

'Irish, no sweat. That boy will go the distance. One of the stand-up guys. So, Aaron, if we're going to check out that Page outfit. See what they pay top Troppo hands, I'd better do something about a ticket.'

'You're serious, Jake? Great. Look, I'm on the next plane going east. What say we see if there's a seat left?'

'Okay. Take me five minutes.'

The big man lumbered away and in a surprisingly short time was back. 'Got it. Toronto, connecting to Washington.'

The waitress arrived and looked relieved when another round was declined.

'You guys going to be all right?'

'Better than ever, honey. Bring the tab. How about you, Doc? Want another?'

'Thanks, Aaron, but I'll pass. The party is about over but how about a rain check?' Doc drained the bottom of the glass and continued. 'Let me know where you land. You got my address. I'm running out of drinking buddies, you know what I mean?'

'Christ, you better not let Amy hear that. She already figures I'm a bad influence.'

Jake was busy restlessly scratching an ear, and at last he said, 'Maybe we better get down there. They'll be calling our flight in five minutes, and I hate that last in line crap.'

'Okay, Jake. I wish you were coming, Doc. Could be a good party.'

'Thanks, buddy, but I can get enough fireworks at home. Nope. I don't think that Viet Nam thing is going to be any minor league scuffle, but let me know. Send a sarong.'

Aaron and Jake drained their glasses and then stood a moment at the side of the table. Doc raised his glass.

'No thigh too high, no muff too tough. Hang loose, gentlemen.'

Doc sat alone, looking across the business below him. The waitress arrived and cleared the table and Doc waved her away when she asked about another drink.

He made preparations for leaving and in a low voice muttered, 'That green grass fever shit. It's not the ice that gets in your blood.'